"Kate, are y⟨...⟩

He seized her by the elbow. "What are you doing here alone on a night like this?"

"You're hurting me," Kate said in a small voice, and Luis released her with a muttered curse. "I'm quite capable of taking care of myself, you know."

Luis shot the bolts on the big doors, then turned to her purposefully. "That is something I think I'll put to the test. Perhaps I should demonstrate what you were inviting had you remained outside alone and unescorted, Kate."

And before she could realize what he meant, he pulled her into his arms and held her there, laughing down into her incensed face before he bent his head to kiss her.

Catherine George was born in Wales and, following her marriage to an engineer, lived in Brazil for eight years at a gold-mine site. It was an experience she would later draw upon for her books, when she and her husband returned to England. Now her husband helps manage their household so that Catherine can devote more time to her writing. They have two children—a daughter and a son—who share their mother's love of language and writing.

Books by Catherine George

HARLEQUIN ROMANCE

HARLEQUIN PRESENTS

BRAZILIAN ENCHANTMENT

Catherine George

Harlequin Books

TORONTO • NEW YORK • LONDON
AMSTERDAM • PARIS • SYDNEY • HAMBURG
STOCKHOLM • ATHENS • TOKYO • MILAN
MADRID • WARSAW • BUDAPEST • AUCKLAND

Original hardcover edition published in 1991
by Mills & Boon Limited

ISBN 0-373-03201-3

Harlequin Romance first edition June 1992

BRAZILIAN ENCHANTMENT

CHAPTER ONE

A TAP on her bedroom door in Fulham was one thing. Here in a hotel in the mountains of Minas Gerais, hundreds of miles from Rio de Janeiro, it was a different affair entirely. Kate threw back her long, damp hair and stood, hairbrush in hand, hoping she'd imagined the timid little sound. But a second knock soon put paid to that idea. She stared at the door, biting her lip. Maternal warnings on the perils of foreign hotel rooms had amused Kate at home. Now none of them seemed remotely funny. Assuring herself that it was merely a chambermaid wanting to turn down the bed, Kate crossed the room to the door.

'Who is it?'

Silence.

Kate frowned, irritated. 'Tony? Are you playing games?'

The knock came again, fainter this time. Kate hesitated, then shrugged, resigned. This was a highly respectable hotel, previously vetted by the school, after all. She opened the door, then dodged back in alarm at the sight of a strange young man leaning against the lintel, his face desperate with entreaty. As he held out a wavering hand Kate gasped in dismay and tried to slam the door in his face but before she could manage it he fell across the threshold face down, unconscious at her feet.

Kate stood rooted to the spot in horror for an instant, her eyes popping out of her head, then she dropped down on quaking knees beside the fallen man. He was young, expensively dressed, and in his present position seemed likely to suffer severe respiratory problems if she left him with his face buried in the bedside rug. Kate steeled herself to heave him over on his side, then let out a screech of fright as her fingers came away sticky with the blood staining his white shirt.

'No—no!' she muttered wildly. 'This can't be happening—I'm having a nightmare——' But a groan from the prostrate man proved her hideously wrong. He very plainly needed help, and fast. Kate jumped to her feet and ran for the telephone beside her bed, somehow managing to piece enough Portuguese together to request the hotel manager's presence in her room immediately. Her voice cracked on the last in a way which must have convinced the receptionist it was an emergency, since in a shorter time than Kate dared hope help arrived in the shape of Senhor Paulo Pedroso, *hoteleiro* of the Pouso da Rainha. The slim, dark Brazilian let out a muffled exclamation, appalled to discover a bleeding, unconscious intruder in the room of a guest he had welcomed only that afternoon to his hotel. Putting Kate gently aside, the hotel manager examined the man swiftly, manoeuvred him carefully so that the door could be closed, then snatched up the telephone and gave several staccato orders. Eventually he was put through to someone he spoke to with great deference, plainly not relishing the task. Afterwards he turned his full attention to Kate, installing her solicitously in a chair before taking a blanket from the bed to cover the unconscious man, all the time apologising to his guest in English which was heavily accented but reassuringly fluent, to Kate's relief. The shock, she found, had numbed her brain too much to cope with a foreign language.

'Mr Morton is not yet returned, alas,' he said regretfully.

At that moment Kate wasn't interested in her colleague, Tony Morton. 'What—what about...?' She waved a hand towards the prostrate figure, her stomach heaving at the sight of the blood oozing sluggishly into the blanket.

'I was instructed not to touch him. His brother will be here very soon.' He looked up as a knock sounded on the door. He opened it a crack, then took a glass of brandy from some unseen hand before closing the door firmly again. He handed the glass to Kate, insisting she drink the spirit straight down.

Kate detested brandy, but since some kind of restorative seemed only sensible in the circumstances she swallowed it down like medicine, shuddering as the fiery spirit did its work.

'Senhor Pedroso, do you know who it is?' she said apprehensively. The injured man's eyes remained closed, and his smooth olive skin had a greyish look about it, but an occasional faint moan indicated he was at least alive, if nothing more. 'Has he been shot?'

'*Sim*, I know him.' The *hoteleiro* looked grim. 'His name is Claudio Vasconcelos, Senhorita Ashley, and he has been stabbed.'

'Stabbed!' Kate's face blanched. She leapt to her feet to peer at the ashen face of her uninvited guest. 'But won't he die if he doesn't get attention very soon?'

'No, no. It is a flesh wound only.' Paulo Pedroso looked up sharply at the sound of screeching brakes in the courtyard below. Seconds later footsteps rapped on the polished board floor in the corridor outside.

'The doctor?' asked Kate.

'No, Miss Ashley.' The *hoteleiro* looked rather tense. 'It is Senhor Luis Vasconcelos, the elder brother of Claudio.'

Kate didn't care who it was, provided he removed the blood-stained, groaning Claudio from her room as quickly as possible. The man who strode into the room took in the scene in one comprehensive glance which swept her from head to foot then ignored her. He slammed the door shut behind him, firing questions at Paulo Pedroso in a peremptory, low-toned voice as he dropped on one knee to examine the unfortunate Claudio.

Luis Vasconcelos was older than his brother, his hair, which for the moment was all Kate could see of a rather well-shaped head, thick and straight, and of an unusual walnut shade quite unlike the dense black of the youth's clustering curls. When he looked up at last Kate was put in mind of other faces she'd seen often enough before in museums, on swarthy men in brass helmets and cuirasses, with hooded eyes which stared down from paintings in heavy gilded frames. The Vasconcelos family, it was evident, was descended from one of those conquistadores who'd presented Brazil on a golden plate to his Portuguese king.

Paulo Pedroso looked on uneasily as the man stared at the dishevelled girl in silence, the cold eyes travelling over her with a deliberation which was an insult in itself. Kate flushed resentfully as he took in her tangled, streaming hair, the satin dressing-gown, the empty brandy glass still in her hand. In one expressive glance Luis Vasconcelos summed her up and dismissed her as beneath contempt. Kate's nails bit into her palms as he brushed aside the *hoteleiro's* attempt to introduce her. Distaste in every line of him, he turned his back on Kate as he stooped to pick up the unconscious body of his brother, muscles rippling under the shirt stretched across his broad shoulders as he took the weight.

'Doutor Costa espera no hospital,' he said tersely to Senhor Pedroso, as he prepared to depart, not even breathing heavily, Kate noted with resentment. *'Obrigad', Paulo.'*

'De nada. Sempre as suas ordems.' The hotel manager, much to Kate's annoyance, appeared to have forgotten her existence entirely as he hurried ahead to summon the lift. Luis Vasconcelos, on the other hand, turned very deliberately to stare at Kate across his limp burden.

'Puta!' he spat, then strode away before she could say a word.

Kate slammed the door behind him, trembling with rage. Who, in heaven's name, did this Vasconcelos man think he was? Or more to the point, perhaps, who did he think *she* was? Certainly not someone worthy of an introduction, for a start, otherwise he'd have soon learned she had nothing at all to do with his wretched brother's mishap. Kate stiffened. Unless he actually thought *she'd* stabbed the wretched Claudio! She paced up and down agitatedly, until the bloodstain on the white rug stopped her in her tracks. Suddenly a wave of homesickness engulfed her. She darted across the room to make sure the door was locked, then slammed the windows shut with trembling hands, wishing Tony would stop exploring Vila

Nova and get himself back to provide her with some moral support.

She dashed away angry tears as a knock sounded on the door.

'Tony?' she called, brightening.

'No, *senhora*. Do not be afraid. It is Paulo Pedroso once more, with one of the maids.'

Disappointed, Kate unlocked the door and let the hotelier into the room, smoothing back her dishevelled hair as he spread his hands in apology.

'Miss Ashley, I most deeply regret the great distress you have suffered.' He beckoned to the maid hovering outside, and at once the girl whisked away the offending rug, then began to straighten the room.

'Did you explain to that—that excessively rude man that I've only just arrived here, that I'd never laid eyes on his brother before in my life?' demanded Kate.

Senhor Pedroso looked very uncomfortable. 'Alas, there was no time. He was in much hurry to get Claudio to the hospital. The doctor awaited them. But Senhor Vasconcelos will soon learn you were not involved.' He gestured about him at the room. 'You will not, I think, wish to sleep here in the circumstances.'

'I certainly don't. Not that I'll sleep much tonight anyway, Senhor Pedroso, after what's happened.' Kate gave him a beseeching look. 'If I *could* move to another room I'd be very grateful.'

'*Pois é*. The rooms on the top floor are unoccupied. You may sleep in one of them undisturbed by fear of intrusion.' Senhor Pedroso looked suddenly uncomfortable. 'Perhaps you would like Mr Morton moved to that floor also?'

Kate flushed. 'Certainly not, Senhor Pedroso.'

The hotelier looked even unhappier than before, his upper lip beaded with perspiration as he made profound apologies once again, reinforcing them with the offer of dinner free of charge. Eventually Kate was moved, not merely to one room but to a top-floor suite comprising bathroom, bedroom and sitting-room, complete with balcony and a view of the entire town of Vila Nova against its backdrop of mountain peaks.

Kate felt a lot better in her new quarters. Fully dressed, with her hair braided into its usual corn-dolly plait, she felt more like herself by the time Tony Morton came racing up the stairs after the surprise of finding she'd been moved to another room.

'You can look but you can't come in,' said Kate firmly, stopping him short in the doorway.

Anthony Morton, a graduate from the same university as Kate, and a working colleague of hers ever since, looked astonished at her greeting. He was slim and fair like Kate, with skin tanned like hers from spring sunshine in Italy, where they'd both been teaching English to Italian employees of a large car factory. Friends for years, neither had any romantic inclinations towards the other. Nevertheless, Tony was not only accustomed to admittance to wherever Kate was living, but in Turin had actually shared a house with her, in company with another man and two girls, all similarly employed.

'Why can't I come in?' he demanded, peering around at the room. 'Got a man in here?'

'Not now I haven't!' She plunged into an account of her adventures with the Vasconcelos brothers. 'It was quite horrible,' she concluded with a shudder. 'I was in a bit of a state after all that, so to calm me down Senhor Pedroso offered to move me up here away from the scene of the crime.'

'Which still doesn't explain why I can't come in,' Tony reminded her.

Kate coloured a little. 'They seemed to think you might be more than just a friend, whereupon I made it clear, in no uncertain terms, that you were merely my colleague. Besides, in this part of the world I gather it's no entry for any male, other than husband or brother, where a lady's bedroom is concerned.'

Tony leaned in the doorway, looking thoughtful. 'You're probably right. I was only a kid when I lived here, of course, but I remember Mother commenting—with approval probably—of the way young ladies were firmly hedged about with protocol in this neck of the woods.'

'So let's not tread on any toes,' said Kate. 'I'm only here by accident in the first place, so the last thing I want is to get any backs up.' She sighed. 'Particularly after getting off to such a disastrous start tonight. My fame, no doubt, will have gone before me before I even start work.'

Tony patted her hand comfortingly. 'Don't worry— come on, let's go down to dinner. You'll feel better on a full stomach.'

'Sorry, love. I'm not very hungry, and to be honest I just can't face the dining-room tonight. I've asked for a tray in my room.' Kate smiled apologetically. 'See you in the morning.'

Tony looked crestfallen. 'Can't I persuade you? No?' He shrugged philosophically. 'OK. Sleep tight, and if any more strange men knock on your door dive for the telephone and Sir Tony will come galloping to the rescue.'

'I'll hold you to that,' Kate assured him. 'By the way,' she added, '*you* speak Portuguese. What does "*puta*" mean?'

Tony's eyes narrowed. 'Where the devil did you hear that?'

'It was the only word Senhor High and Mighty Vasconcelos actually addressed to me personally—by way of a parting shot, as it were.'

'Did he, by George?' Tony looked grim. 'Not exactly the sort of word one learns at Mother's knee, you know. It means—well——'

'Daughter of joy?' suggested Kate delicately.

Tony grinned. 'More or less! I'll certainly have a word to say to this chap Vasconcelos if I run into him.'

Kate shrugged. 'You won't run into him. He's pretty obviously one of the local bigwigs. You and I, Tony dear, are most unlikely to move in such exalted circles.'

As predicted, Kate found it very difficult indeed to sleep that night. Weary and hot-eyed, she tossed and turned for hours, unable to get the older Vasconcelos brother out of her mind. It was a new experience to see contempt in a man's eyes when he looked at her. If all men in this part of Brazil were like him, she thought acidly, it was a great pity she'd ever come here. She'd been so excited, too, over taking the place of poor Phil Holmes, the man originally chosen for the job. When Phil had gone down with appendicitis at the last minute Kate had jumped at the chance of a trip to Brazil.

She slept at last, but woke early to a dawn chorus of cockerels. Yawning, Kate slid out of bed and went out on the sitting-room balcony to admire Vila Nova in the soft light of a new day. The hotel, built in

Portuguese colonial style, was situated on the out-skirts of the town in gardens ringed with eucalyptus trees, and from her vantage point on the third floor Kate had a panoramic view of Vila Nova in the distance. As the sun rose higher she could make out twin-towered churches and houses with cinnamon roofs and walls which glimmered palely among tall palms and other greenery less easy to identify.

Kate leaned against the balcony rail, enchanted by the prospect before her. She would not, she vowed, allow last night's events to cloud her pleasure in this pretty little town of Vila Nova. From now on she was determined to make the most of her opportunity to teach in this impressive country, *and* enjoy it. No one else she met, surely, could possibly be as disagreeable and insulting as the unfriendly Mr Vasconcelos.

After breakfast the two English teachers were to be collected by Senhor Julio Alves, the commercial manager of Minvasco SA, a large local company which numbered coffee and wine among its exports. Kate and Tony were required to teach English at top speed to a small group of employees destined to man the company's new UK commercial outlet in London.

No problems there, at least, reflected Kate. She very much enjoyed teaching English as a foreign language. Her pupils always learned quickly and eagerly, happy under her tutelage. Admittedly they were always adults eager to learn, instead of children who weren't; nevertheless Kate was well aware that she had a natural talent for instilling a workaday, serviceable knowledge of English into her pupils in record time. Tony had been first choice for this particular job, of course, because he spoke Portuguese, though anything but

English was strictly forbidden during the short, concentrated sessions of instruction.

When Kate went down to breakfast Tony was there before her. 'Did you sleep?' he asked.

'Eventually.' She sighed. 'Despite my delightful accommodation, and a very comfortable bed, I had problems dropping off, I'm afraid.' She smiled at the hovering waiter, told Tony she'd like fruit, toast and coffee, then listened with admiration as he reeled off her order.

'Perhaps I'll learn a bit as I go along,' she said hopefully. 'Though it seems a lot more difficult than Italian.'

'You'll soon pick it up. I absorbed it sort of by osmosis when I was a kid,' said Tony cheerfully. 'Learned it from the maids and the gardener.'

'Servants! How grand.' Kate grinned.

He shrugged, and tucked into the sizzling platter of eggs and crisp, smoked bacon put in front of him. 'Not really. Everybody who worked for Dad's outfit had servants and a biggish house.'

'Why on earth did your parents leave, then?'

'To educate me.'

'I hope it was worth it!' Kate gave him a teasing smile, then applied herself to the *compote* of mangoes and pineapple set before her. 'What's on today, then?'

Julio Alves had rung Tony the previous evening to confirm that after breakfast he would escort them into Vila Nova to the offices of the Companhia Minvasco SA, where they would be presented for inspection to the *Patrão*, the big white chief, who would then graciously allow them to proceed to the brand-new school he'd had built just outside the town.

'It's not even finished yet—I had a look at it on the way back last night,' said Tony, pouring coffee. 'We are to function, I gather, in the kindergarten, which was completed only last week. The *ginásio* building—secondary school to you—is still under construction, so we may well have to compete with concrete mixers as we teach.'

Kate was undismayed by the prospect. 'I've got a good pair of lungs—and we work a lot with pictures anyway.' She glanced down at herself. 'If we're to meet this *Patrão* person——'

'The boss-man himself, in case you're wondering.'

'I'd gathered that.' Kate looked across at Tony questioningly. 'Perhaps I ought not to wear trousers. What do you think?'

'Sweetheart, it's a sin to wear trousers with a pair of legs like yours anyway, but it's up to you.' Tony thought for a moment. 'On the other hand I wouldn't mind betting things are still fairly conservative here in the interior, so perhaps a skirt might be a good idea at that.'

Kate drank down her coffee and got up quickly. 'OK. Give me ten minutes. I'll meet you in the foyer.'

As she passed the reception desk the manager came to intercept her, greeting her solicitously. '*Bom dia*, Senhorita Ashley. I trust you managed to sleep a little last night? Were the new rooms satisfactory?'

'Good morning, Senhor Pedroso. The rooms are quite lovely,' she assured him blithely.

'You have recovered from your fright?'

'Oh, yes.' She smiled brightly. 'I'm sorry I made such a fuss last night.'

'*Não, não*, you were very brave,' he contradicted fervently. 'I pray that the remainder of your stay will be both peaceful and enjoyable.'

Amen to that, thought Kate, as she speedily replaced her denims with a dark blue linen skirt. She knotted a blue silk scarf at the throat of her crisp white cotton shirt, slid her bare brown feet into low-heeled navy leather shoes, then eyed her hair. Perhaps this *Patrão* person, who was likely to be fairly elderly if he was head of a company like Minvasco, might consider a plait a bit juvenile for someone hired to teach his employees. Kate unravelled the braid, brushed her hair back smoothly, securing it at the nape of her neck with a tortoiseshell clasp. The Italian sun had gilded her fair hair with lights which made a pleasing contrast with her narrow, tanned face and the eyes which, Kate knew very well, were her best feature; large and dark-lashed, of an unusual shade somewhere between dark grey and violet, with a luminous clarity which was a major part of their attraction.

'You look terrifyingly tidy and efficient,' said Tony, when she rejoined him.

Kate laughed, amused by a similar transformation in her companion. Tony had opted for uncharacteristic formality with white shirt and college tie, worn with a lightweight blue suit.

'Dad says first impressions are important,' said Tony sheepishly. 'Thought I'd put my best foot forward just for today, at least. Once we're actually teaching I'll revert to normal.'

When the commercial manager arrived to collect them Kate was glad they'd both elected to dress formally. Julio Alves, a black-moustached man in his late thirties, was immaculately dressed in a beige linen suit, his black shoes reflecting the sun which poured down as he led them to his car outside in the courtyard. His English, though eccentric and heavily accented, was more fluent than Kate had expected. She was able to converse very readily as they were transported smoothly in a large Mercedes, a chauffeur at the wheel, while Senhor Alves made polite enquiries as to the comfort of their accommodation, and asked about their first reactions to his part of Brazil.

Once Tony revealed he'd lived in Minas Gerais before, Senhor Alves was soon deep in conversation about Tony's childhood before moving on to the inevitable football, a subject never far from any Brazilian's heart. Kate was left to her own devices to gaze through the window at the town. Vila Nova, she realised, was built on a series of ridges, with breathtakingly steep streets, many of which were cobbled. The houses she'd seen from a distance earlier proved to be not quite so immaculate on closer inspection, but very attractive for all that, with shops and bars sandwiched among private dwellings, a square here and there, one with a vegetable market overlooked by one of the twin-towered churches, where locals could be seen wandering in to pray as part of the daily routine of their lives.

Eventually the car stopped in a tree-shaded square in front of an eighteenth-century building built in the now familiar colonial style, complete with ornate pillared portico and shutters at every window.

'O edificio Minvasco,' announced Senhor Alves as he handed Kate out of the car with a flourish.

She looked up at the building in surprise. It looked more like a relic of bygone municipal glory than the offices of a modern company like Minvasco.

'*Very* grand,' she murmured to Tony, as they crossed the black and white mosaic pavement to enter a large hall with several doors leading off it, all labelled with the names of their occupants.

'Impressive,' he agreed as they mounted a staircase which ascended in a pair of graceful curves to the upper floor. Julio Alves tapped on one of the rosewood double doors set dead centre at the top of the stairs, then ushered Kate and Tony into an ante-room and reception area which served a main office hidden beyond yet another pair of impressive doors. A young male clerk spoke rapidly to Julio Alves, who asked Kate and Tony to sit on chairs which were remarkably like genuine Louis XIV gilt and brocade *fauteuils*. Senhor Luis, he informed them, was for the moment engaged in a telephone conversation with his brother in Parana. He would not keep them waiting long.

Since the commercial manager then excused himself to talk with the young clerk, Kate had time to examine her surroundings with interest.

'Not short of a penny, this Senhor Luis, would you say?' she said in an undertone.

'I'll say! Minvasco must be a pretty successful company,' agreed Tony.

In addition to the valuable chairs they were sitting on, there were several oil-paintings of superb quality on the walls. Everything in the room was of the same high standard. No wonder Minvasco could pay to hire English teachers, thought Kate.

A few minutes later a buzzer sounded on the intercom, and Julio Alves came across the room to say the *Patrão* was ready to receive them.

'Should we touch our foreheads to the floor as we go in?' muttered Kate under her breath, and saw Tony's lips compress to smother a snort of laughter as they were ushered into a room which contained only a few chairs, a very large desk, and a man. The latter had been seated behind the desk as they went in, but as he caught sight of Kate he sprang to his feet precipitately, his eyes incredulous as he stared at the slender fair girl advancing towards him between her two male escorts.

Kate would have sold her soul to turn tail and run, her blood running cold at the discovery that the *Patrão* of the Companhia Minvasco SA was none other than the man she'd last seen staring at her in disgust across the body of his unconscious brother.

CHAPTER TWO

'Posso apresentar-lhe a Senhorita Ashley é o Senhor Morton——' began Julio Alves with very creditable fortitude in the circumstances, since it was obvious that his employer was gripped by an emotion powerful enough to paint angry slashes of colour along the cheekbones of his olive-skinned face.

'Que bobagem é isso, Julio?' interrupted Luis Vasconcelos harshly, staring in disbelief at Kate.

Trying to ignore her trembling knees Kate forced herself to look him straight in the eye. 'Do you speak English, please?' she said very precisely. 'I'm afraid I don't understand Portuguese.'

Tony looked swiftly from Luis Vasconcelos to Kate in dismay. 'Kate?' he said urgently. 'Was this . . .?'

She nodded briefly, while Julio Alves, who plainly wished himself a thousand miles away, took it on himself to explain that this was the lady and gentleman who had come to teach English to the *Patrão's* employees.

Oblivious of the others, Luis Vasconcelos addressed himself scathingly to Kate. 'You? Give lessons in *English*?' he said, making it insultingly clear that the only lessons he believed Kate capable of were in a different field altogether.

Kate bristled, her colour a match for his, and Tony put a restraining hand on her arm as he launched into a flood of Portuguese which Kate, although unable to follow, assumed was an attempt to clear up the

21

misunderstanding. Luis Vasconcelos, his attention turned to Tony for the first time, heard him out with rigid courtesy before his eyes returned to Kate's blazingly angry face.

'Your friend appears to be unaware of your acquaintance with my brother,' he observed glacially, and held his hand up as Tony tried to interrupt. 'Please.' With a courteous nod he indicated that his commercial manager's presence was no longer necessary. Once Julio Alves had departed, with very obvious relief, Luis Vasconcelos waved the other two to a pair of high-backed chairs in front of his desk. 'Please be seated.'

'I'll stand,' snapped Kate.

'If you do not sit your companion must remain standing also, *não é*?'

Stormy grey eyes clashed with dark implacable ones, and after a moment Kate sat, allowing Tony to do the same.

'I do not wish to refer to the events of last night,' began Luis Vasconcelos coldly. 'They have little to do with the fact that I requested two male teachers for the English lessons. The fact that you, Miss...?'

'Ashley,' said Tony quickly.

'That you, Miss Ashley, are female comes as an unwelcome surprise. I was expecting a Mr Philip Holmes.' The dark eyes turned in Tony's direction. 'Why did this Mr Holmes not arrive?'

Unhappily Tony explained why Kate had been substituted for his male colleague at the last moment. 'The school informed Senhor Alves,' added Tony.

'I see. I have been in Parana. I did not return until the evening of yesterday.' Once again the cold dark eyes locked with Kate's. 'Last night certain events sent all thoughts of English teachers from my mind. I therefore did not learn that a *lady* had been selected to take the unfortunate Mr Holmes's place. Particularly one so well-acquainted with my foolish young brother.'

At which point Kate arrived quite suddenly at the end of her tether. 'Until he barged into my room and collapsed at my feet last night I had never laid eyes on your wretched brother. And I won't stay here to be insulted a moment longer, Senhor Vasconcelos,' she added bitterly. 'Please tell Senhor Alves to make the necessary arrangements for me to leave at once.' And without a word to Tony she swept from the room.

Tony came rushing out after her, catching her by the hand. 'Look, Kate, there's no point going off half-cocked like that. If you and Vasconcelos will only simmer down we can get to the bottom of this business with his brother in no time——'

'It won't make any difference,' Kate reminded him furiously. 'I'd still be a "lady" instead of the *man* he wants so much. Maybe his sexual preference lies in that direction. You'd better watch out if you stay on.' She looked up to see Luis Vasconcelos in the open doorway, his face a rigid mask of affront.

Although he'd obviously heard the insult he ignored Kate as he summoned Julio Alves with an imperious hand. 'Please escort Miss Ashley back to the hotel, Julio, then take Mr Morton on a tour of the school, *por favor*. You will then please arrange a return flight to England for Miss Ashley on the first plane available.'

The clerk, who had been speaking on the phone while Luis was giving orders, caught his employer's eye.

'*É Senhor Pedroso para senhor—é muito insistente,*' he said apologetically.

Luis Vasconcelos excused himself with swift, indifferent courtesy, and strode into his office, slamming the doors behind him.

The journey back to the hotel was unhappy. Tony spent most of it trying to persuade Kate, in an urgent whisper so Julio Alves and the driver couldn't hear, to let him go back to Luis Vasconcelos and tell him she'd been a mere innocent bystander the night before. Kate, in the grip of anger greater than anything she'd experienced in her entire life before, hissed at him to shut up and mind his own business, in a manner so foreign to her normal, equable self that he subsided miserably and did as she said.

At the Pouso da Rainha, Julio Alves handed Kate out of the car with great formality, telling her she would be informed of the requisite arrangements for her return flight by late afternoon. Kate thanked him with even greater formality, thawed sufficiently to give a tiny smile to Tony, then walked with rigid dignity into the hotel.

As Kate passed the dining-room there was a sudden hiatus in the buzz of conversation between waiters laying tables for lunch. All eyes turned in her direction for an instant before the young men hurriedly resumed their task. Kate breathed in deeply, trying not to mind, then the pretty receptionist came running from behind her desk, rather surprising Kate by the warmth of her smile.

'Senhor Paulo wishes to talk with you, *senhora*, if you please. He begs that you have coffee with him in his office.'

Kate nodded, smiling, wondering how the manager had known she'd be back so early as she followed the girl to a small room at the rear of the main foyer, where Paulo Pedroso sat behind a desk, a young woman near by at another, typing furiously. He rose to his feet and shook hands with Kate formally across the desk.

'Senhorita Ashley, please sit down.' He gestured to the girl at the typewriter to stop working, then told the receptionist to order coffee. 'This is Rosa,' he said, indicating the typist, who smiled shyly. 'You do not mind if she remains here while we talk? It would not be—polite for me to entertain you alone. I fear some of our customs must seem strange to you.'

Kate shook her head, returning Rosa's smile. 'Not at all, Senhor Pedroso. I feel one should abide by local customs—wherever one happens to be.'

The arrival of a tray provided a little diversion, and as Kate drank the strong, delicious coffee she felt the hard, tight knot of anger in her chest beginning to loosen a little.

'Have you heard how the invalid is today?' she asked anxiously. 'My intruder of last night, I mean?'

The *hoteleiro* nodded gravely. 'This is why I wished to speak with you. I feel much responsibility for what happened.'

'It wasn't your fault, Senhor Pedroso,' Kate assured him.

He gave a wry smile. 'In a way, I fear it was, Miss Ashley. I regret that Claudio Vasconcelos was stabbed by one of my chefs.'

Kate's eyes opened wide. '*Really?* Good heavens, why?'

Paulo Pedroso shrugged, exchanging a look with Rosa. 'To understand why it is necessary to know Claudio, Miss Ashley. Perhaps last night you were too distressed to see that he is very——'

'Beautiful!' put in Rosa with fervour.

Kate smiled involuntarily. 'No, I'm afraid his looks didn't register much. I was too taken up with the blood all over him.' She frowned suddenly. 'You're not telling me he's——?'

'No, no, *senhora*.' Paulo Pedrosa smiled reassuringly. 'Today Claudio is recovering well. *O médico* was obliged to make a few *pontos* . . .' He frowned. 'Stitches, is that right?'

'For the wound? Yes.'

'For the rest, Claudio is young and in excellent health, and after a day or two in hospital he will be little worse.'

'Good,' said Kate, relieved, then eyed him curiously. 'But why did your chef stab him?'

'Sofia!' blurted Rosa, then blushed.

Her employer gave her a quelling look as he explained that Sofia had been employed at the Pouso da Raina as a chambermaid on the recommendation of her *noivo*, her fiancé, the chef. Sofia, possessed of considerable good looks, had caught the susceptible Claudio's eye one day when he came to lunch at the hotel, with the inevitable result. Filled with burning ambition to better herself, the girl had set her sights on a husband from the wealthy Vasconcelos family instead of a mere chef. There had been illicit meetings, notes passed in secret . . .

'How did you know all this?' interrupted Kate, fascinated.

Two pairs of dark eyes regarded her with surprise.

'It is not possible to conduct such an affair in Vila Nova in secret,' said Paulo Pedroso simply.

Kate frowned. 'Then why didn't Claudio's brother know about it?'

'He has been away, *senhora*, visiting the Minvasco holdings in Parana. Otherwise matters would not have progressed so far. Luis Vasconcelos would not countenance an alliance between his brother and a girl like Sofia.'

Snob, thought Kate, then paid close attention to the rest of the story. Yesterday, it seemed, Claudio had left a note in the usual place, a certain tree in the gardens of the hotel, arranging to collect Sofia at the end of her shift. Unfortunately the vengeful chef had intercepted the note and lain in wait. When Claudio had come to a side-door of the hotel at dusk he had found Manoel instead. The chef, armed with one of his own carving knives, had stabbed Claudio expertly, in a way intended to punish rather than kill. The victim had then been dumped in the service lift and dispatched to Kate's floor while the chef had made his escape with the terrified Sofia.

'Claudio staggered from the lift as far as your room, *senhora*,' concluded the *hoteleiro*. 'The rest, *infelizmente*, you know very well.'

Kate regarded him in silence for a moment. 'Thank you, Senhor Pedroso. But it's still a mystery to me that Senhor Vasconcelos—Claudio's brother, I mean—imagines *I* was involved.'

The *hoteleiro* looked deeply embarrassed. '*É minha culpa*, Miss Ashley—my fault. Senhor Luis was naturally much disturbed by the plight of his young brother. He was in no mood to listen to explanations. But I did not know he had never seen Sofia. It did not occur to me that he would mistake *you*, *senhora*, for one such as she.'

Kate went up to her room feeling slightly better now she knew that Luis Vasconcelos was in possession of the facts. Not, she thought balefully, that she would stay and teach his precious employees now if he went on his aristocratic knees and begged her. The school would just have to send someone else—a male someone else at that—to fit the *Patrão*'s requirements.

The pretty, airy rooms on the top floor seemed a haven. Kate freed her hair, shaking it loose as she went out on the balcony to turn her face up to the sun. Here in June it was halfway through the cold season in these spectacular mountains, but at this time of day the sun was hot and the air crystalline, the sky so deep a blue that no artist's palette could have reproduced it. Kate breathed in deeply, rubbing at her tense neck muscles as she leaned against the balcony rail, depressed and suddenly deeply resentful that her stay in this beautiful region was to be so brief. Curse Luis Vasconcelos! The only people pleased by all this would be her parents, who hadn't wanted her to come so far to work in the first place. Kate smiled wryly, thankful they knew nothing of the previous night's little adventure.

Kate stayed where she was at her balcony rail, her face raised, letting the sunshine wash over her in a warm, soothing tide, until at last she found that she quite fancied some lunch, and went back into the room in time to hear a tap on her door.

'Kate! Are you there?' called Tony.

He looked like a cat full of stolen cream, his eyes shining with a mixture of triumph and excitement as Kate opened the door to him.

'Let me in,' he ordered. 'I've got news for you.'

'You can't come in, remember!'

'Oh, rubbish, Kate——'

'Nothing doing.' Kate closed the door behind her and locked it. 'You can tell me over lunch.' She paused, eyeing him. 'Unless, of course, you've got a better offer?'

Tony shook his head, seizing her arm in a punishing grip as he almost ran with her down the stairs. 'Of course not—in any case I was bidden to have lunch with you so I could give you the glad news.'

Kate stared at him. *'Bidden?'*

He grinned. 'Well, it did rather come across like that. He's a natural with the orders, isn't he?'

'Who?'

'Luis Vasconcelos, of course!'

Kate detached her arm crossly, resisting an urge to snap Tony's head off as they were shown to a window table in the dining-room. There was a frustrating interval while starched napkins were shaken out by two attendant waiters, ice-water poured for them, rolls and butter provided, small dishes of *crudités* presented for them to nibble before they were finally left in peace to study menus printed in Portuguese and French.

Tony pushed his aside, unable to keep his news to himself any longer. 'Everything's OK now, Kate. You can stay.'

Kate stared at him for a moment, then went on studying the menu.

'Did you hear what I said?' hissed Tony.

'I heard.'

'Well? What do you think?'

Kate considered. 'I think I'll have the prawns in garlic dressing, and a salad.'

Tony ground his teeth. 'Haven't you been listening to me, girl? I said you can *stay*!'

'I know. You didn't, however, ask me if I wanted to.'

Tony regarded her in blank astonishment until a polite interruption by one of the waiters forced him to make a choice from the menu. Once they were alone again he returned to the attack.

'Are you mad, Kate? After all the trouble I've gone to on your behalf, you ingrate! Instead of inspecting the school I persuaded Julio Alves to take me straight back to Vila Nova so I could convince the *Patrão* of Minvasco that, not only were you an innocent by-stander in that mess his brother got into last night, but also the best damn teacher he could possibly have if he's keen on getting his chaps to speak English P.D.Q.'

'Despite the impediment of my sex?' said Kate maliciously, crunching on a carrot stick.

Tony grinned. 'That was the difficult bit. But someone seemed to have had a talk with our Luis before I got there, because he rather climbed down from his high horse and admitted that now he was in full possession of the facts he much regretted the distress caused to Senhorita Ashley.' Tony shrugged. 'He didn't say what the facts were, though, so I still don't know who attacked his brother.'

'*I* do. But never mind all that now. What did he say about the teaching bit?'

Luis Vasconcelos, it seemed, had not been altogether delighted to be put so entirely in the wrong as far as the Senhorita Ashley was concerned. It had taken a palpable effort on his part to admit his mistake, and to give consent for Kate to remain to teach his employees.

Kate was prevented from a blistering reply by the arrival of her prawns, which were suspended, plumply pink and luscious, round the rim of a glass goblet of dressing sunk into a silver bowl of ice.

'What a work of art! I thought I was ordering a prawn salad,' she said in surprise.

'You get the salad afterwards as a main course,' said Tony, attacking his bowl of soup with relish.

'What did you order?'

'*Canja*, soup made with chicken and rice, followed by a *bife*—minute steak reeking of garlic—served with black beans and rice. I was brought up on this sort of thing. Wonderful!'

Since Tony had no attention to spare for anything but his soup for the moment, Kate made herself eat all her prawns, along with a slice or two of thin brown bread, before she ordered him to finish his story. Laying down his spoon, he smiled at her smugly, saying that his glowing recommendation of her talent as a teacher had won the day, along with one other finicking detail which had finally convinced Luis Vasconcelos.

'And what was that?' asked Kate, glowering.

'Julio Alves got in touch with the school in London and found they had no one free to come out in place of you for another six weeks, dear heart!'

'What a pity,' said Kate sweetly, as she began on a salad which was an artistic mixture of every salad vegetable she'd ever seen, plus a few she hadn't, garnished with slivers of chicken, garlic sausage and curls of pink ham.

Tony eyed her uneasily. 'What are you getting at?'

'Eat your steak—dear heart.' Kate smiled at him, her eyes darkened to violet with satisfaction. 'All I meant was that it's *such* a pity no one can come out to take my place, because I wouldn't stay to work for Luis Vasconcelos if he paid me a diamond a day and went down on his knees to beg.'

And nothing would move her, despite the efforts made by Tony as he walked Kate round and round the hotel's picturesque gardens, arguing his head off in an attempt to persuade Kate to stay.

'Not,' he said flatly at one stage, 'that I can picture Luis Vasconcelos on his knees in any circumstances. You're more likely to get the diamonds than have *that* gentleman crawling to you.'

Kate shrugged. 'It's all quite academic anyway, Tony. I'm not staying, and that's that.'

Tony failed to change her mind; no matter how much he reminded her that in Italy they'd occupied a self-catering flat, which, though they'd enjoyed their time there, could hardly compare with Vila Nova, where they were being put up at a very comfortable hotel and fed like kings.

But even though Kate had no intention of staying she was very curious to look over the new school with Tony. Julio Alves proved to be a very enthusiastic guide as he held forth on his employer's aim to provide the young of Vila Nova with a comprehensive education from kindergarten to late teens.

'Some will then be prepared for jobs, others for the university,' he said with satisfaction. 'It has always been Senhor Luis's goal to return into the community some of the wealth enjoyed by his family over the centuries.'

'Centuries?' asked Kate, startled.

Julio, with some pride, informed her that one of Senhor Luis's ancestors had been a *companheiro* of the Pedro Alvares Cabral who had first set eyes on the Brazilian coast and claimed the land for Portugal. A later Vasconcelos, on finding gold in this region of Minas Gerais, built the town which he named Vila Nova de Vasconcelos, to give it its full title.

Secretly very impressed, Kate said very little as she accompanied the two men on a tour of the school building, part of which was still surrounded by sand and cement mixers and piles of bricks, with dark-skinned men in hard hats skimming up and down scaffolding as the construction progressed. The kindergarten, which was separate from the main building, was a one-storey construction, ready except for tiny chairs and tables. One of its classrooms had been prepared for the English lessons, furnished with full-size desks and chairs, a dais and a lectern set up in front of a wall with a large section of blackboard.

'This,' announced Julio Alves with pride, 'is where you teach.'

Tony was emphatic with his assurances that everything was very satisfactory.

'And you, Senhorita Ashley?' enquired the Brazilian. 'Do you find the conditions suitable?'

Before she could reply Kate saw his eyes focus on a point behind her, and turned to find that Luis Vasconcelos had joined them.

So far her encounters with Luis Vasconcelos had been so tense and emotive on both occasions that Kate had a picture in her mind of a swarthy, scowling ogre.

The man regarding her now looked very different. With no contempt to mar his clear-cut features, Luis Vasconcelos was unquestionably a very attractive man. If Claudio's supposed to be the beautiful one, she thought with detachment, he must be really something.

'Good afternoon, Miss Ashley,' he said, nodding to Tony and Julio Alves. 'Julio, perhaps you would be so good as to show Senhor Morton over the part of the building still under construction. He will, I am certain, find our building methods of much interest.'

'I would indeed,' said Tony promptly; keeping his eyes firmly averted from the glare Kate directed at him as he went off with Julio Alves, apparently blind to the fact that the last thing she wanted was to be left alone with Luis Vasconcelos.

CHAPTER THREE

'I FEEL sure it's against local rules for me to remain here alone with you like this,' said Kate, carrying the war into the enemy's camp.

Luis Vasconcelos waved a hand at the windows which made up three of the walls enclosing them. 'You are in no danger here, where all who wish may look on.'

'I was thinking of the danger to my reputation, rather than to my person!'

'Miss Ashley, there is no cause for concern. Neither you nor your reputation risk any harm from me, here where all may see, or otherwise.' The eyes holding hers, Kate noted, now she had more leisure to inspect them, were a surprisingly light, tawny brown. The impression of darkness came from the thick black lashes which fringed them. 'I desired this time alone with you,' he went on, 'to make apology for the unfortunate misunderstanding last night.'

Kate said nothing. She glanced away very deliberately, looking through the windows towards the half-built part of the building.

'I bore you, Miss Ashley?' said her companion acidly.

Her eyes flashed dangerously as she turned back to him. 'Senhor Vasconcelos, you were insulting and objectionable to me, both last night and this morning. You flatly refused to listen to any explanation of the terrifying situation your brother landed me in. I'm not *bored*. I'm furious.'

His lips tightened. 'I am aware that my behaviour must have caused you much distress——'

'Distress!' snorted Kate.

'My choice of words is not always perfect to express what I mean in your language,' he said stiffly. 'What I try to say is that I wish to make reparation.'

'The only reparation necessary, Senhor Vasconcelos, is a return ticket on a plane to England tomorrow—with a full explanation to my employers as to why.'

'I have come here to persuade you to stay,' he said, his face mask-like.

Her mouth curved in a scornful little smile. 'Really? And I know why!'

His eyes narrowed. 'You do?'

'I'm not stupid! The school doesn't have someone to replace me right away, while you, I gather, need two teachers as of now.'

Luis Vasconcelos shrugged. 'That is true, of course. I require my employees fluent in time for the opening of the new London outlet. Nevertheless, the reason I wish *you* to stay, Miss Ashley, is that I am told you are the best possible teacher, male or female, for the task.'

Kate's eyebrows rose. 'You mean you're willing to take Tony's word for it?'

He smiled faintly, throwing out his hands. 'Alas, I confess it was not Mr Morton who convinced me. He, I know well, is your good friend. He would naturally be prejudiced. No; I contacted your employers myself. Your recommendation came straight from the horse's mouth, I think you say. They were most insistent that you remain.'

Kate looked away, deflated. Now, she thought, mortified, she'd have to swallow her nonsense about diamonds and Luis Vasconcelos on his knees. Good though she might be at the job, if she dashed back to London without even starting the present one the language school might think twice before employing her again. Which would be a shame, because she enjoyed both the teaching and the travel. And, if she was honest, she was utterly captivated with Vila Nova. She *wanted* to teach in this dear little school, *and* see something of a part of the world she might never see otherwise.

But it meant swallowing her pride as well as her words. On the other hand, she reminded herself, Luis Vasconcelos had managed to swallow *his* pride to apologise, which, she was willing to bet, was a pretty rare event in his life. Besides, now that she was able to look back on the evening before more objectively, she could see that his mistake had been understandable enough, even if his reaction had been so objectionable. No man finding his brother in such a state could be blamed for... Are you making excuses for him? she asked herself, and smiled wryly. The excuses, of course, were for herself, in a way; a means of letting herself back down.

'You smile?' asked Luis Vasconcelos quickly.

Kate turned to look at him. 'Yes. A private joke, Senhor Vasconcelos.'

'I had hoped it was a sign that you had decided, in spite of last night, to stay.'

'Even though I'm a woman, not a man?'

His face blank of expression, Luis Vasconcelos nodded. 'Even so, Miss Ashley. Some things I am powerless to change.' His eyebrows rose in question. 'You have decided?'

She looked at him levelly for a moment or two, then nodded. 'Now I've given it more thought I don't really have any alternative.'

'I am glad. My apology was very sincere, Miss Ashley.'

'It may have been, but it wasn't the deciding factor, Senhor Vasconcelos.' Kate gave him a cynical little smile. 'I'm staying purely because I'm worried I might lose my job if I don't!'

He looked amused. 'You are very honest.'

'I try to be.'

'It is not a quality all women possess.'

'Nor all men, either.'

He bowed gracefully. '*É verdade*. Now, having granted me one wish, Miss Ashley, will you grant yet another by accepting an invitation to dine at my house tonight? Mr Morton also, of course.'

Kate's instinct was to refuse, but something in the way he was looking at her, as though he could read her mind, changed it for her. She smiled at him politely. 'How very kind. Thank you.'

'It is my pleasure.' He hesitated, his face darkening suddenly as he threw her a questioning look. 'Miss Ashley, has Paulo Pedroso told you exactly what happened to my brother last night?'

'Yes.' Kate bit her lip, flushing. 'I'm so sorry. I've been rude. I haven't even enquired how your brother is—though Senhor Pedroso assured me it was only a flesh wound.'

'It is no more than Claudio deserves.' Luis Vasconcelos gave a very expressive shrug. 'He is lucky it was no worse. Perhaps it will teach him to leave other men's women alone in future.'

'What will happen to the chef?'

'Since Claudio wronged the man by seducing his Sofia I do not blame Manoel for his revenge.' His eyes narrowed. 'Not, Miss Ashley, that I take lightly such treatment of one of my family.'

Kate looked at him in surprise. 'But won't you bring charges against the man—or whatever you do in this country?'

'No. Since Sofia accompanies him on his search for work elsewhere I consider him punished enough.' The tawny eyes gleamed with sudden irony. 'What worse fate can a man suffer than to possess an unfaithful woman for wife?'

'I thought they were only engaged.'

'The lady in question, I have learned, is happy to marry her chef after all, now that her hopes for marriage with my brother are dead.' The wide, expressive mouth curled contemptuously. '*Estúpida!* As if one such as she could trick her way into my family.'

'Because she's just a chambermaid?' said Kate sharply.

Luis Vasconcelos looked at her with hauteur. 'Not so! I would, I admit, prefer a wife with more intelligence for Claudio, but it is not Sofia's humble birth I despise—merely her lack of morals.' He glanced towards the window, then held out his hand to Kate. 'I see Julio bringing Mr Morton to join us, Miss Ashley. I shall send a car to the Pouso da Rainha at eight-thirty, if that is convenient.'

Kate touched his fingers briefly. 'Perfectly, Senhor Vasconcelos. I look forward to it.'

'I don't see diamonds,' said Tony, eyeing Kate that evening in the small bar. 'And don't tell me Luis Vasconcelos went on his knees, begging you to stay, because it won't wash, so what did the trick, Catherine Ashley?'

Kate shrugged. 'I have, as you well know,' she said with a sigh, 'rather a tendency to fly off the handle. Long before Luis Vasconcelos apologised for assuming I was his brother's ambitious little bimbo I realised that not only would I like to stay in these parts for a while, but that the school would object pretty strongly if I went straight back to England without giving a single lesson, particularly when pro tem there was no one to send in my place, male *or* female.'

Tony grinned. 'And is *Senhor Patrão* now reconciled to the fact that you're undisputably of the latter persuasion?'

Kate tasted her glass of local wine with appreciation. 'Mmm, this is rather nice.' She gave Tony a reproving look. 'Even people like Senhor Vasconcelos, *Patrão* of Minvasco, and probably monarch of all he surveys, can't change some things. He needs a couple of teachers quick and, for the moment, you and I are the only ones on offer. As he said himself, some things you can't change.'

'Like my suit,' said Tony gloomily. 'You females are lucky. Here we are, about to taste of the Vasconcelos fleshpots, and the only improvement I could make to my appearance was a shower, shave and a change of shirt. Whereas you, sweet Kate——'

'Happen to be wearing the one halfway suitable thing I packed.' Kate grinned. 'Well, Mother packed it, actually. I didn't think I'd need anything very fancy, but she insisted I put this in with the rest.'

'This' was a narrow skirt and cropped, collarless jacket in heavy violet silk, worn over a silvery satin camisole, the subtle shades very flattering against Kate's eyes and hair.

'Why,' said Tony casually, looking into his glass of lager, 'do you suppose we've been invited into the lion's den tonight?'

Kate shrugged. 'To make amends, I suppose, for all the fuss last night.'

'It didn't concern *me*.'

'True. But the *Patrão* could hardly invite me without you, could he?'

'Unflattering, but true.' He eyed her moodily. 'Watch your step, Kate. This isn't Fulham, remember.'

'How observant, Tony dear!'

'You know what I'm getting at, Kate.' His blue eyes were rueful. 'I've known you a long time, and, well, I'm used to the fact that you're warm and friendly, and just a bit flirtatious now and then—doesn't mean a thing. In this neck of the woods, love, it might just be misunderstood.'

Instead of flaring up, as Tony obviously expected, Kate looked at him in silence for a moment, her eyes considering. 'You mean I should preserve utter propriety at all times when in company with the local male populace.'

'Exactly.'

Kate saw the receptionist beckoning and picked up her bag. 'I'll do my very best, old love. And if, as I strongly suspect, you're referring to Senhor

Vasconcelos himself, don't worry. He's not the sort one *can* get very friendly with, is he? Even supposing I had any disposition to do so, which I do not. So come on, get a move on. Our chariot awaits.'

Kate was sorry it was dark as they were driven out of Vila Nova in the now familiar Mercedes along a road which led away from the town to wind upwards in dizzying curves towards the top of a tree-crowned hill. Moonlight illuminated the road, it was true, but she would have liked to see the Vasconcelos family home in the bright light of day. In the black shadows and bright silver light there was an air of unreality about the entire place. Tall gates opened by courtesy of some unseen hand as the car approached and Tony whistled softly as they drove on through gardens filled with flowers and palms before the driver stopped the car beside an ornate stone fountain in front of a house not unlike the Pouso da Rainha. This house, however, was bigger, grander, and much older; a piece of eighteenth-century Portugal set down in perfect reproduction in the interior of Brazil.

Tony took Kate by the arm as the driver left them standing before the great double doors of the house. 'Nice little place,' he murmured.

Kate nodded dumbly. Tony's little homily had been quite unnecessary, she thought with irony. A man who lived in a place like this would never dream of coming any nearer than arm's length. It wouldn't occur to someone like Luis Vasconcelos to think of her in any way other than as the girl he was paying to teach his employees English.

A smiling maid admitted them into a cavernous hall floored in marble, its walls inlaid with pastoral scenes depicted in *azulejos*, the blue and white tiles of

Portugal. Dim light from an iron candelabrum fell on Chinese porcelain arranged on dark carved chests beside Goanese sofas with insets of wicker and faded brocade seats. Brooding, imperious faces stared down from heavy gilded frames on a carved wood staircase which ascended in majesty into the shadows of the upper floor.

'It's a museum,' whispered Kate, overwhelmed.

'And here comes the master of the house,' said Tony, *sotto voce*, as Luis Vasconcelos appeared on the staircase, descending to greet them with out-stretched hand, his smile lighting features which bore a marked resemblance to those in the portraits he passed on his way down.

'*Bem-vindo.* Welcome to you both.' He raised Kate's fingers to his lips then shook Tony by the hand warmly before leading them across the hall into a room which was a complete contrast, full of comfortable chairs and small tables and what seemed, at first glance, to be hundreds of potted plants.

'This is known as the garden-room,' said Luis Vasconcelos, and smiled. 'Both because it has one wall of glass, as you can see, and leads straight into the garden, and because of my mother's obsession with hot-house plants of all kinds.'

'It's charming,' said Kate, cheered by the room's informality after the culture shock of the entrance hall.

'It's very good of you to invite us here tonight,' added Tony, looking oddly young and less sure of himself in the company of his host, who wore a dark suit of such masterly elegance that Kate was thankful for her violet silk.

'I am grateful for your company,' said Luis Vasconcelos courteously. 'I regret that my mother is not here to add her welcome to mine, but for the moment she is in Parana, where my *cunhada*—my brother's wife—is soon to present her with a third grandchild. But please, allow me to offer you a drink.'

Kate, despite a sudden desire for something strong as an antidote for uncharacteristic nerves, asked for mineral water, feeling she might need her faculties in mint condition during the evening ahead.

Tony, a little diffident at first, began to relax as he praised the school their host was building, then went on to embarrass Kate by lauding her proficiency at the type of teaching required to get the Minvasco employees fluent in colloquial English at top speed.

'She had the best success-rate of us all in Italy,' he declared, as he sipped from a very tall glass of gin and tonic, blandly ignoring the black look Kate sent in his direction.

'I am fortunate, then,' said Luis Vasconcelos smoothly, 'that fate has conspired to send Miss Ashley here to Vila Nova.'

'Despite your preference for a man,' Kate couldn't resist saying.

'Even so.' He shrugged. 'You must forgive my prejudice, Miss Ashley. Here in Vila Nova we are not as emancipated as in London. You will find our society, I fear, far more male-orientated.' He looked up at the sound of the doorbell. 'Ah! That will be the other guest. Forgive me—I will leave you for a moment to welcome her.'

Her? Kate made a little face at Tony. 'There's been no mention of a wife, so can we be about to meet the *noiva* of the *Patrão*?'

'*Noiva?* You *are* coming on with the Portuguese.'

'It's one word I'm not likely to forget, is it, after my brush with Claudio Vasconcelos?'

Tony laughed, then rose to his feet as their host reappeared with a lady who, whatever else she might be, was certainly not the fiancée of Luis Vasconcelos. She was tall and rather angular, with greying blonde hair upswept into a faultless chignon, and her age could have been anywhere around the fifty mark. She smiled with great warmth as Luis Vasconcelos escorted her through the obstacle course of tables and plants.

'Miss Ashley, Mr Morton, allow me to present Senhora Marques,' he said, smiling at his companion as she shook a reproving finger at him.

'Now, now, Luis, stop teasing,' she said, in accents of ineluctably London origin. She smiled at Kate and Tony mischievously, obviously revelling in their surprise. 'I may be Senhora Marques these days, but I was once plain Connie Parker, from Camberwell Green. He tells me you two are going to teach some of his lads to speak English. I could have done it for him, of course, but he didn't fancy my Cockney accent!' She threw a laughing glance at Luis, who returned it affectionately, to Kate's surprise.

'*Mentira!*' he declared. 'You lie, Connie. You did not wish to teach!'

'Of course I didn't, but never mind me,' said Connie Marques eagerly, and sat herself down beside Kate. 'I'm dying for news from home.'

Both Kate and Tony were instantly captivated by the unexpected guest, who displayed such genuine interest in their homes and families and crowed with astonishment when she learned that Tony had spent part of his childhood in Brazil.

'So you're like me, love,' said Connie Marques, accepting a glass of wine from her host with a sunny smile. 'A bit of a mixture. I'll always be a foreigner here, of course, but when I go back on holiday to London I find I'm a bit of a foreigner there now, too. Neither fish, fowl nor good red herring as you might say!'

'Do you have any family here, Senhora Marques?' asked Kate.

'Oh, yes, dear, only don't bother with that "Senhora" stuff. Just call me Connie.' The fair, rather bony face shadowed a little. 'I'm a widow now, more's the pity. My José died five years ago.' She smiled determinedly. 'But I've got Linda, my daughter. She's married to a doctor in São Paulo, so I don't see as much of her and my two gorgeous little grandsons as I'd like, but I've got lots of friends here in Vila Nova, and Luis and Claudio drop in to see me now and again, and I come up here to see their mum, Dona Francisca, when she's in residence.' Her blue eyes sparkled wickedly. 'We both belong to a bridge circle and give teas, you know. Imagine it! I never thought I'd learn to play bridge in English, yet now I can beat the socks off most people round here in Portuguese!'

In company with the irresistible Connie, as she thought of her from the first, the constraint Kate had experienced at first in Luis Vasconcelos's imposing home vanished completely over the dinner table, despite the fact that they ate from priceless plates and drank wine from the Vasconcelos vines in Parana. She would not, she vowed silently, let herself be overawed.

With Connie Marques's encouragement both Tony and Kate talked about the time spent in Italy, and their college days before that. Luis Vasconcelos, it occurred to Kate, was very clever. By inviting the friendly, informal Connie, he was learning far more about his English teachers in an hour or so than he'd have done in a month of Sundays if he'd entertained them alone.

'This dish is not to your taste, Miss Ashley?' he asked quietly, as the other two laughed together.

Kate smiled politely. 'It's perfect, Senhor Vasconcelos. The entire meal is delicious. Your chef is an artist.'

He grimaced. 'Do not talk of chefs, if you please. At this moment I feel very *antipático* towards the breed!'

Kate smiled. 'Tactless of me. I'm sorry.'

'You are mistaken also, Miss Ashley. We possess nothing so grand as a chef at Casa dos Sonhos.' He waved a slim brown hand at the dishes left on the table within reach. 'All this is prepared by Lidia, the cook who has been with my mother since before I was born.'

'She's to be congratulated. Do you have a lot of servants?'

His eyes met hers narrowly. 'Is there a note of censure in such a question?'

'None at all,' Kate assured him. 'I was merely curious to know how many people are needed to keep a house like this in smooth running order.'

Connie looked up from her conversation with Tony. 'Are you talking about servants, dear? Dona Francisca told me that when she came here as a bride there was an army of them.'

'No longer, I fear,' said Luis. 'Including Lidia, a small force only now.'

'I only vaguely remember the servants my parents had,' said Tony, plainly feeling a need to pour oil on troubled waters. 'But my mother never tires of saying how the maids spoiled me rotten.'

'They love children here,' said Connie, looking a little sad. 'I never managed more than one, and that was a daughter——'

'Did that matter?' asked Kate swiftly.

'No, love. Not in the least. José adored her. But all men want a son, don't they, Luis?'

The arrival of the next course saved their host from a reply he plainly had no wish to make, and gave Tony the chance to fix Kate with a disapproving blue eye.

After the meal, in the more relaxing atmosphere of the frankly cluttered garden-room, the conversation became general, with a lively discussion on current world affairs followed by a wistful catechism from Connie about the latest West End successes.

'That's the thing I miss most, really,' she said with a sigh. 'I used to love to go up West to a good play or a musical. *And* I used to haunt the second-hand bookshops! I just love a good book.'

'So does Kate,' said Tony with a grin. 'She brought loads of the damn things. The case I lugged around for her weighed a ton!'

'I'll lend you anything you like,' Kate assured the other woman, smiling. 'The new PD James is good—I read it coming over in the plane.'

'You have made a friend of Connie for life, Miss Ashley,' said Luis Vasconcelos, offering brandy. 'She would rather read than eat, I think—or even play bridge.'

Kate refused brandy in preference to the delicious coffee which Connie informed her also came from the Minvasco holdings in Parana.

'Lovely, isn't it, dear? I took some home with me last time, but it didn't taste the same at all in London. Different water, Luis says. My old mum thought it was horrible. Prefers her jar of instant.'

There was general laughter at their host's expression of distaste, particularly when Kate informed him that her English degree would never have been possible without instant coffee, plus the cheeseburgers and yoghurt of her staple diet as a student.

'It is surprising that bright eyes and so beautiful a complexion result from such ill treatment,' said Luis Vasconcelos suavely.

Kate flushed bright red and there was a sudden, awkward silence which Connie Marques broke by jumping up to take Tony by the hand.

'Come and hear the crickets sing under the eucalyptus trees, Tony. It's as bright as day outside.'

Tony eyed Kate doubtfully. 'How about you?'

'I desire a word in private with Miss Ashley,' put in Luis Vasconcelos blandly. 'It will not take long, I promise.'

Kate was apprehensive at the prospect of a tête-à-tête with her host, who settled himself in a nearby chair with the air of a man prepared for battle.

'I assume,' she said challengingly, 'that it was your idea for Senhora Marques to take Tony outside.'

'That is correct, Miss Ashley.' He took out a thin silver cigar case, asked her permission, then lit a cheroot before embarking on a conversation he plainly expected to be difficult.

'I asked you here tonight to meet Connie Marques for a reason,' he said, eyeing her through a blue spiral of smoke.

Kate nodded, resigned. 'Yes. I assumed we were all here for some specific purpose, rather than a mere social occasion.'

'Not so Mr Morton—Tony. I invited him from courtesy only.'

She looked at him in silence, waiting for him to go on. He took his time, choosing his words with care.

'My dismay at learning a female teacher had been sent here was in no way personal, Miss Ashley, despite the disaster of our first meeting.' He smiled very faintly. 'Nevertheless, the fact that you are a woman teacher for a class of men is not an ideal situation. To command respect from them everything they know of you must be above reproach.'

'Caesar's wife,' said Kate acidly.

'*Exactamente.*' He got up and strolled to the open door, blowing a blue stream of smoke out into the night. 'To ensure that no one doubts your— your——'

'Virtue?'

He swung round, the corners of his mouth quirking. 'This is difficult for me, you understand. I would explain so much better in my own language. To be brief, I am afraid it is impossible for you to remain alone at the Pouso da Rainha.'

Kate's eyes darkened ominously. 'I'm *not* alone there, Senhor Vasconcelos. Tony's there too.'

'Miss Ashley, it is Tony's very presence that is part of the problem.' The patrician face took on a remote look. 'If you remain at the hotel alone with him, all will assume that your relationship is more than just professional.'

'But I'm not alone with him! The hotel's full of other people.'

'*Pois é.* But not one of them is *solteira*, a single lady. You are very beautiful, Miss Ashley. To remain at the hotel means, I fear, that you run the risk of male overtures you will find distasteful. And, since you are my personal responsibility while you remain in Vila Nova, I have arranged for you to move from a hotel to a private house for the duration of your stay.'

'You're not suggesting I move in *here* by any chance?' said Kate hotly.

Luis Vasconcelos looked down his nose at her. 'You misunderstand, Miss Ashley,' he said, the urbane host suddenly replaced by the autocratic *Patrão* of Minvasco. 'It is not my practice to invite single ladies to stay at Casa dos Sonhos when my mother is away. I refer to the home of Senhora Marques, which is not only charming but conveniently situated not far from the site of the new school. She has been kind enough to offer you accommodation in her home.'

Mortified by her gaffe, Kate poured herself more coffee with an unsteady hand. 'I see. What about Tony?'

Luis Vasconcelos's face took on a look of weary patience. 'He will stay at the Pouso da Rainha. As any *male* colleague of his would have done also.'

'I see.' Kate digested the news thoughtfully for a moment or two, then rose to her feet. 'Then if that's all, Senhor Vasconcelos, I think it's time I went. Thank you for a superb meal. Tony and I will start work at nine in the morning.'

Luis Vasconcelos looked taken aback. 'So soon? Do you not wish some time to accustom yourself to the altitude here? Perhaps you are not aware that we are higher in Vila Nova than your mountain of Snowdon in Wales. Newcomers tire easily at first.'

'Very true,' said Kate, with a delicate little yawn intended to convey boredom rather than fatigue. 'In my case more than usual. After what happened on my first night in Vila Nova I seem prone to insomnia.'

He threw up a hand like a fencer, acknowledging the thrust. 'It was most regrettable, and I apologise yet again. Claudio, also, will apologise when able to do so. But it must convince you of the need to move from the hotel. I am sure that under Senhora Marques's roof you will sleep more easily.'

Kate's little shrug expressed her doubt eloquently. 'Will someone pick us up in the car in the morning?'

'*Pois é*. I will send Dinis with the car to the Pouso da Rainha for Mr Morton, after which he will proceed to the Casa Londres to collect you on the way to the school,' he assured her blandly.

'You mean I'm expected to move out of the hotel tonight?' she said, dismayed.

'It would be best, yes. Connie will help you with your packing, and the car will wait to take you to her home.' The tawny eyes held hers. 'I have already informed Paulo Pedroso, Miss Ashley. He is in possession of my wishes.'

'You mean orders, Senhor Vasconcelos!'

A sudden, transforming smile lit his eyes. 'Very possibly, Miss Ashley. As I said before, my command of your language is not always what I would wish.'

'On the contrary,' said Kate. '*Command* is no problem at all for you, Senhor Vasconcelos—in your language or mine.' She smiled brightly as Tony reappeared with Connie Marques, looking so hunted that it was obvious he knew about the new arrangement. 'Right, then, Tony. Time we were going. We start work first thing in the morning.'

Tony blinked. 'I thought we started on Tuesday.'

Kate shook her head. 'I'm sure Senhor Vasconcelos can sort out some pupils for us by nine in the morning. The sooner we start, remember, the sooner we can finish what we came for and get back where we belong.'

There was an awkward little silence.

'Right, fine,' said Tony hurriedly, and held out his hand to his host. 'Thanks for a great evening.'

'*De nada*. Please come again soon.' Luis Vasconcelos turned to Kate. 'You also, Miss Ashley. A welcome awaits you at Casa dos Sonhos at all times.' He held out a slim brown hand, and Kate touched hers to it briefly as she echoed Tony's thanks with unsmiling formality.

'Such a lovely name for a house, isn't it?' said Connie hurriedly.

'Very unusual,' agreed Tony. 'Is there a story attached?'

'It was the name chosen by the ancestor who built it,' said Luis Vasconcelos as they walked through the hall. 'His intention had been to make a speedy fortune, then return in triumph to Portugal. But he fell in love with a local beauty who feared to leave her native shore. Unable to part from her, he built this replica of his family home here in the heart of Minas, and abandoned his dream of returning to Portugal. To commemorate this fact he named his new home Casa dos Sonhos—House of Dreams.'

CHAPTER FOUR

THE home of Constance Marques, née Parker, proved to be a rambling, one-storey house set back from a quiet road in a garden full of flowers bleached uniformly white by the moonlight.

'I don't blame you for feeling fed up at having to move in with me,' said Connie apologetically as she got out of the car to a tumultuous welcome from a dog which came hurtling through the moonlight towards them, yelping in delight as he jumped all over Connie. The yelps changed to growls at the sight of Dinis, the driver, who deposited Kate's suitcases hurriedly and took to his heels to gain the safety of the car. By the time the fuss had died down, and Connie had introduced the new house guest to Bruno, the German Shepherd, Kate was feeling thoroughly ashamed of herself.

'I've been very rude, and I'm deeply sorry. I'm delighted to move in with you, Connie,' she said sincerely, as she located the exact spot which Bruno liked scratched behind his ear. 'You're very kind to take me in. I only hope it's not too horribly inconvenient.'

'Inconvenient!' Connie gave a little squawk of laughter. 'Goodness, love, you're a godsend not an inconvenience. I get a bit lonely now and again, you know. I'm glad of a bit of company. Now, leave that dog alone and come on in the house.'

'Can't he come too?'

'No fear. He's got a nice comfortable bed in the outhouse round the back.'

Kate bade a lingering farewell to Bruno before following Connie along a veranda wreathed in bougainvillaea into a house with polished board floors, furnished with an odd mixture of the exotic and the homely. Dark, carved chairs lived alongside comfortable sofas, pictures with religious subjects hung next to English water-colours, with a needlework sampler worked by Constance Parker, aged ten, in pride of place over the fireplace. There were cushions and books and flowering plants in profusion everywhere, the cosy atmosphere of Casa Londres very different from Kate's first impression of the home of Luis Vasconcelos.

'José insisted on the name because of my being a Londoner,' said Connie with a smile, as she showed Kate into a pretty little guest-room. 'Quite a card he was, full of nice little touches like that.' She looked wistful for a moment, then hurried off to make tea.

As Kate unpacked for the third time in two days she simmered with resentment, convinced that Luis Vasconcelos considered her suite at the Pouso da Rainha too pricey to waste on a mere female, and that whatever he was paying Connie Marques was sure to be a lot less than the hotel price list. None of which applied to Tony, of course, for the simple reason that he was a man.

'I hope,' said Kate, as she rejoined her hostess in the *sala*, 'that you're being suitably reimbursed for putting me up.'

Connie looked amused. 'I wouldn't take a penny, love.'

Kate stared at her, appalled. 'You mean you're doing this for Luis Vasconcelos for *nothing*?'

'That's right. And only too glad of the chance.'

'But you're being exploited!'

Connie roared with laughter. 'You sound just like my old dad. No exploitation about it, I promise.' She sobered, waving a hand at her surroundings as she explained that Casa Londres was a company house, the property of Minvasco.

'When José died, Luis Vasconcelos had every right to ask me to leave, you know,' said Connie. 'I thought once about going back to Camberwell, but I couldn't bear the thought of being six thousand miles away from my Linda and the boys, and when Luis heard from his mother that I wasn't keen to go he said I could live in the house rent-free for the rest of my life. Which is why I jumped at the chance of doing something for him in return—especially when he told me you were English!'

Feeling rather deflated, Kate drank her tea in thoughtful silence. At last she looked at the other woman in appeal. 'I can't help feeling *I* should pay for my keep, though, Connie. Won't you let me contribute something for what I eat, if nothing else?'

'Not a chance, love.' Connie smiled reassuringly. 'Just having that pretty face around for a while will be payment enough, I promise. Now what time do you want to be up tomorrow?'

When Kate joined her hostess next morning just before eight she found Connie enthroned behind a coffee-tray at the breakfast table, perfectly made up, every hair in place as she consulted with the maid, Elsa, who was a plump, dark-skinned girl in a print dress and white apron, her teeth showing in a wide white smile as her mistress introduced her to the *'professora Inglêsa'*.

'That sounds terribly grand,' said Kate with a grin, as she sat down to coffee and toast with Connie.

'Not a bit of it. You're a teacher and you're English, aren't you?' Connie eyed her young guest's face. 'Sleep all right, love?'

Kate smiled ruefully. 'Not especially. The bed's wonderful and the room's charming, but I probably found it a bit hard to settle because it's the third change of scene in as many days.' And fantasies about giving Luis Vasconcelos his come-uppance hadn't helped much, a fact Kate thought best to keep to herself since Connie was obviously the man's number one fan.

When the car arrived to collect her Kate was ready, looking neat and appropriate in a grey linen skirt and crisp cotton shirt, her hair tied at the nape of her neck with a white-printed grey silk scarf. Tony lounged, yawning, in the back seat, attired in his usual uniform of denims, thin cotton shirt and navy sweater as the chauffeur helped Kate into the car.

'Obrigada,' said Kate with a brilliant smile for Dinis.

Tony's eyebrows went up as she slid in beside him. 'Soon be chattering like a native at this rate.'

'Hardly. I can say about six words so far and recognise a few more—one of which,' she added darkly, 'I hope never to hear again.'

'You and Vasconcelos don't exactly hit it off, do you?'

'No.' Kate gave the lounging figure beside her a disparaging look. 'I notice he didn't move *you* out of the Pouso da Rainha. Only me.'

'You know why! He's only protecting you, Kate.' Tony eyed her questioningly. 'Aren't you comfortable at Dona Connie's?'

Kate looked a trifle shamefaced. 'Yes, of course I am—she's a sweetie. It's just that I resent being pushed from pillar to post like so much baggage. Luis Vasconcelos should have consulted me first about the move instead of handing me over to Connie like a pound of tea.'

'Perhaps he thought it would save argument,' said Tony, yawning again.

'I do hope I'm not boring you!'

'Not in the least. I just feel so damn sleepy. Mother said I would. You, on the other hand,' he added, 'look as bright as a button. The altitude doesn't seem to be affecting you at all.'

'The altitude is the least of my problems.' Kate looked a little tense as they arrived at the site, where the day's construction was already well under way. 'I hope our pupils aren't all clones of the *Patrão*, bristling with animosity towards a mere female.'

'No one,' said Tony flatly, as he helped her out of the car, 'could ever describe you as a "mere" anything, Kate. So brush that chip off your shoulder, for crying out loud, and let's get on with the job.'

The small kindergarten looked positively crowded when Kate entered the classroom. Not only were there six young men waiting for the arrival of the *professora Inglêsa*, but to her intense dismay the tall, elegant figure of Luis Vasconcelos stood at the lectern on the platform, glancing at his watch impatiently, as though they were late instead of a good ten minutes early.

'*Bom dia*, Miss Ashley, Mr Morton,' he said with brisk courtesy, giving each of them a slight bow. 'I decided to come in person to present my employees to you.' And without further ado he reeled off a list of names as Kate shook hands very formally with one man after another, all of them dark, some more attractive than others, but all of them with a common expression of intense interest in their eyes as they came face to face with the English girl hired to teach them her language. Tony, with his usual easy manners, deflected their attention unobtrusively after a while, chatting to the group in Portuguese to their surprised delight, giving Luis Vasconcelos the opportunity to draw Kate aside.

'You are very silent this morning, Miss Ashley.'

'This type of teaching precludes any greeting other than English, Senhor Vasconcelos,' she informed him. 'I shall speak to my class only when I begin the lesson.'

'You permit that I stay to watch for a while?'

Kate's eyebrows rose. 'If you can spare the time.'

'I should not, *de certeza*, but I am curious to see how these so very expensive lessons work.' He shrugged. 'I am a businessman. I like to receive value for money.'

'As you wish. It's immaterial to me, Senhor Vasconcelos, whether you stay or not.'

'So very hostile still,' he murmured, his face expressionless. 'You have not forgiven my mistake.'

She favoured him with a straight, unsmiling look. 'Which one, Senhor Vasconcelos?' Then she turned to mount the dais, directed a friendly smile towards the expectant faces upturned towards her and said, 'Hello!'

Kate waited until she received a 'hello' in response, then smiled approvingly, waving a hand to indicate that each man should seat himself at a desk. Then she took a bundle of large photographs and magazine cuttings from her briefcase.

Tony tacked them to the blackboard, handed Kate a pointer, then retreated to stand with Luis Vasconcelos while Kate began her first lesson with the aid of a picture depicting a telephone. After half an hour her pupils knew the word for each part of the instrument, how to answer when it rang, what to say when making a call, and were all so caught up with Kate's enthusiasm that they were soon vying with each other to volunteer the correct terms, and, what was more, pronouncing the English words with a creditable attempt at reproducing Kate's clear, unaccented diction.

Immersed in her teaching as always, Kate soon forgot she had any audience other than her pupils, and two hours passed swiftly before she smiled at her class and dismissed them for a half-hour break. She turned to Tony with a sigh of relief.

'Phew! How did I do?'

'You were great. As usual!'

She grimaced. 'It was a bit nerve-racking at first with Superboss looking on, but I forgot him after a while. How long did he stay?'

Tony looked amused. 'About half an hour. I think he was quite impressed.'

'Relieved his money wasn't being wasted, you mean!' Kate accepted a cup of coffee gratefully from a tray which Tony told her would be provided as often as they liked by the caretaker of the school building.

'I think,' said Tony, 'Vasconcelos was ever so slightly miffed you didn't notice when he left.'

'What was I supposed to do? Curtsy?'

'Now, now, Kate. I'm pretty sure the *Patrão* put in an appearance this morning to make sure proper respect was paid to the lady teacher.' Tony gave a wry grin. 'I think the group got the message loud and clear, don't you?'

Kate poured herself more coffee. 'I would have managed just as well without him.'

'I'm not so sure. When you tripped into the room there were some wolfish gleams in those lads' eyes, I assure you, but one look from the boss put paid to any of *that* right away.'

Kate shrugged. 'I'm sure there was nothing I couldn't have coped with, *Patrão* or no *Patrão*.'

'Well, you don't have to cope any more this morning. There's a nice little staff-room next door where you can prepare this afternoon's session while I take our lads through some grammar and tenses.'

It took Kate only a short time to establish a strong rapport with her pupils, who were all bright, intelligent young men not only eager to learn, but full of excitement at the prospect of working in England, and very conscious of their good fortune in being chosen for the job by the *Patrão*, who, to Kate's surprise, and carefully concealed pleasure, rarely let a day go by without calling in at the school. Luis Vasconcelos, it seemed, felt it was wise to monitor his employees' progress.

'It does no harm for them to know I keep watch,' he remarked, as he drank coffee with Kate and Tony in the staff-room. 'They know that if they do not work well there are many others only too eager to take their place.'

'Frankly,' murmured Tony to his coffee-cup after Luis had taken his departure, 'I think he likes to keep watch on Kate, too, don't you?'

Kate glared. 'Why? To make sure I'm up to the job?'

'No, you shrew! I merely meant he likes looking at you, Kate. Most men do,' he added, laughing as he dodged the ruler she flung at him like a javelin.

Kate was secretly very flattered by Tony's theory about Luis's visits. Her initial resentment and animosity towards the latter had long since faded, and on the days he didn't put in an appearance she missed him far more than she admitted, even to herself. Their talks together, even though strictly business and always in company with Tony, were often the high-spots of days which soon settled into uneventful routine. Each morning she was driven to the school, each day she ate a cold lunch in the staff-room with Tony, and once the day's teaching session was over Dinis dropped her off at the Casa Londres then took Tony on to the Pouso da Rainha.

'Pretty dull for a bright girl like you,' commented Connie towards the end of the second week. 'You must be bored stiff, love.'

'I could never be bored with you around, Connie,' Kate assured her hostess. 'Though I must admit it's a bit different from Italy. No one seemed to think it strange there if one went out on a date. Some of my pupils were very nice men, and amazingly correct. I was wined and dined and delivered back to my digs with polite thanks for the pleasure of my company, then my escort, who was more often than not pretty gorgeous, went home to his mother. In the part of

Italy I was in everyone seemed to live at home until they got married.'

Connie nodded approvingly. 'Nothing wrong with that, either. It's pretty much the same in Vila Nova.'

'Don't you ever get bored yourself here?' asked Kate curiously.

'Sometimes. But I've got quite a lot of friends— I've even had a proposal of marriage. But I couldn't fancy anyone else after José so I turned the chap down.' The blue eyes twinkled. 'Besides—he couldn't play bridge!'

Since Elsa the maid went home at five each day, Kate insisted on helping to wash up after dinner each evening. Afterwards she often watched television with Connie if there was an American movie on it; otherwise Kate found programmes in Portuguese a bit much for her at the end of a day which was never less than demanding.

At the end of the second week Connie decided to invite Tony round for dinner.

'Last weekend he was all right, of course, because he went off to visit his parents' friends in Campo d'Ouro, but he'll be glad of an hour or two with us this Sunday. Or maybe Saturday night. I'm sure Luis won't mind if I have the boy round for a meal.'

Kate's eyebrows shot into her hair. 'Does it matter if he *does* object? Surely you can do as you like in your own house!'

Connie laughed, not in the least offended. 'Of course I can—though it's his house really, you little spitfire. It's just that I promised him I'd look after you.'

Kate shook her head in despair. 'I'm a big girl, Connie. You don't *have* to look after me.'

'You know what I mean, love. As far as I'm concerned you're my responsibility and that's that.' Connie looked up at the sound of barking. 'Sounds as though we've got a visitor.' She peered through the window. 'Well, I never, it's Luis!' She hurried out on the veranda, her face bright with welcome.

Kate pulled a face, wishing she was wearing something more fascinating than old jeans and a sweater, then shrugged philosophically. She made herself stay where she was, curled up on the sofa, as a beaming Connie led her visitor into the room.

'Luis was passing and thought he'd drop in to see us, dear.'

Kate smiled politely at Luis Vasconcelos, hiding her surprise at the sight of him. She'd never seen him dressed in anything but formal, beautifully cut suits before. Tonight, however, he looked different, younger, in a roll-neck sweater and cord trousers in dark green, his zippered jacket in thin soft suede the colour of champagne.

'Good evening, Miss Ashley,' he said with a faint smile. 'I trust I do not intrude.'

'Of course you don't intrude,' said Connie before Kate could utter a word. 'How about some of that Scotch I brought back from London, Luis?'

'*Obrigad*', Connie. How can I resist such an offer?' He turned to Kate as Connie hurried off to get the drinks. 'You must allow me to congratulate you, Miss Ashley. The lessons go well.'

Kate swung her feet to the floor and sat erect. 'Thank you. Our pupils usually learn quickly, Senhor Vasconcelos. It's one of the benefits of teaching by concept.'

'That sounds very technical, Miss Ashley.' He shrugged out of the jacket and laid it down on a chair. 'Have I your permission to sit down?'

'Of course,' she said distantly, rather put out when he settled himself on the small sofa beside her.

'What is this concept method?' he enquired affably, half turned towards her.

Kate edged away a little. 'Teaching with the aid of pictures, to put it into simple terms.'

'Simple terms are necessary for someone like me, who is not as fluent as he would wish in your language.' His eyes were bright with something Kate couldn't quite categorise as they met hers.

'Your English is admirable, as you well know, Senhor Vasconcelos.' She gave him a bright, social smile. 'Where did you learn it?'

'I studied business methods in your country when I was younger. My father was alive then. I spent some time in Europe before returning to apply what I had learned to Companhia Minvasco. Unfortunately,' he added, 'my brothers did not have my advantage.'

'Have you many brothers?' she asked politely.

'Two only, Miss Ashley. César, who is two years my junior, runs the Parana holdings. Claudio, *infelizmente*, you have already encountered.' The handsome face darkened. 'He is much younger, a fact which leads my mother to spoil him. He must have time away from home to grow up.'

'Is that wise?' said Kate involuntarily. She shrugged as she saw the question in his eyes. 'I mean if he's prone to trouble right here under your nose wouldn't he get into worse mischief somewhere else?'

'Perhaps that might be good for him. Here I am always available to rescue him. He might grow up faster if he had only himself to rely on, *não é*?' He frowned, his eyes on her hair. 'It is wet, your hair?'

'A bit damp still. I washed it before dinner.'

'It is a very different colour when dry. The first time I saw you I thought you were *morena*—brunette. Is that the word?'

Kate's eyes glittered coldly. 'I'm amazed you noticed my hair at all that horrible night. You hardly looked at me.'

The corners of his wide, mobile mouth turned down. 'I would give much to have you forget our first meeting, Miss Ashley.'

'So would I. But certain aspects of it refuse to be forgotten. Particularly the one word you flung in my direction.' Kate felt a warm glow of satisfaction as colour rose along his cheekbones, and for a moment Luis Vasconcelos seemed lost for words.

'Here we are,' said Connie cheerfully, coming in with a tray. 'Oh, thank you, Luis. Yes, put it down on that little table. Sorry I was so long. Had to search high and low for some soda. Help yourself to whisky.' She smiled at Kate. 'What about you, love? I brought orange juice, gin, tonic water—or I could open some wine.'

Kate accepted a glass of orange juice, then sat as far as possible from Luis on the sofa as he answered Connie's questions about Claudio.

Claudio, Luis informed them with a wry smile, was perfectly well again and making life at Casa dos Sonhos hell for all because he was confined to the house until his stitches were removed.

'What's he going to do now he's finished in college?' asked Connie.

'Do?' Luis looked surprised. 'He will work for Minvasco, what else?'

She nodded approvingly. 'It's time someone took some of the load from your shoulders.'

A smile lit the black-lashed eyes. 'It will be a long time before Claudio is capable of doing that! *De certeza*, I was telling Miss Ashley only a moment ago that it might be wise to send Claudio away for a while.'

'Stand on his own two feet,' agreed Connie. She shot a wry glance at Luis. 'Does Dona Francisca know about Claudio's little accident?'

Luis shuddered, and took a hasty swallow of whisky. 'No, *graças a Deus*, she does not. Nor will she learn of it if I can prevent it. I have sworn him to silence—the maids also. But it will be a miracle if she remains in ignorance, *sem dúvida*. You know how it is here.'

'Even I'm beginning to know what it's like here,' put in Kate quietly. 'Does everyone in Vila Nova know about *my* part in Claudio's little escapade?'

'If they do, Miss Ashley,' said Luis with authority, 'they know well that you were an innocent victim of his folly. But,' he added with emphasis, 'now that you are safe under this roof you have no cause for concern. Senhora Marques is held in great esteem by all in Vila Nova.'

'There at least,' responded Kate evenly, 'I'm in complete agreement.' She smiled affectionately at Connie. 'She's the best landlady I ever had!'

Connie laughed, then firmly led the conversation into less abrasive channels, and rather to her surprise Kate found that she was enjoying herself very much as she listened to reminiscences of bygone days in Vila Nova. An hour flew by before Luis Vasconcelos glanced at his watch and exclaimed, jumping to his feet as he apologised for staying so long.

'Not long enough,' Connie assured him.

'Nevertheless your guest must be tired after her demanding day!'

Kate shook her head, smiling at him with genuine friendliness for the first time. 'I don't get half as tired as Tony, for some reason, even though he's lived at this altitude of yours before.'

'Then do you think you will enjoy your stay here, Miss Ashley, despite a less than fortunate introduction to Vila Nova?'

Kate smiled. 'I'm very lucky to be here with Connie, of course, and my class is progressing by leaps and bounds, which is great. But I haven't seen anything of Vila Nova itself, so I'm not in a position to judge.'

Luis Vasconcelos eyed her questioningly as he shrugged into his jacket. 'It is in my power to change that, if you wish. It is the reason for my visit tonight—not,' he added, with a bow to Connie, 'that I need a reason, other than the pleasure of the company.'

'Get away with you!' Connie patted his glove-soft sleeve. 'What did you have in mind?'

'Since tomorrow is Saturday, and Miss Ashley and Mr Morton have no lessons, I thought I might lend you Dinis and a car so that you can make a journey of exploration. If,' he added, turning to Kate, 'this would please you, of course.'

Kate's eyes lit up like lamps. 'It would please me very much, and Tony too, I know—if it's OK by Connie.'

Connie was only too delighted with the arrangement, and gave profuse thanks to Luis, who kissed her on both cheeks as he prepared to leave, then shook Kate's hand in his usual formal way.

'I shall send the car for you at ten in the morning, then. I hope you enjoy your day, Miss Ashley.'

'Thank you very much, Senhor Vasconcelos. I'm sure I shall.' Kate smiled at him radiantly.

He gazed at her expressionlessly for a moment, then gave her a formal little bow and went with Connie to the door, pausing for a moment as she held it open for him. 'I almost forgot, Connie,' he said casually. 'There was another reason for my visit. My mother telephoned earlier and asked me to give you a message. César and Pascoa are now the proud parents of a third son.'

Connie made the expected exclamations of delight, which Luis listened to with courtesy before he bade both ladies goodnight and went out into the moonlight to an excited greeting from Bruno, as the dog escorted the visitor to his car.

CHAPTER FIVE

'THAT was a nice surprise,' said Connie, as she rejoined Kate in the *sala*.

'Very nice.' Kate gathered up glasses. 'Let me make you some tea.'

'You're an angel. I'd love some.'

When Kate took the tea-tray back to the *sala* Connie was staring into space. 'What's up, Connie? Something wrong?'

Connie's smile was melancholy. 'No. Not really. I was thinking of Luis.'

Kate's eyebrows rose as she filled two cups. 'Why the glum face? I thought you'd be pleased about the trip tomorrow, not to mention the new little Vasconcelos.'

Connie gave a little shrug as she accepted her cup. 'The idea of the outing's lovely—quite a treat for me, as well as for you, love. It was the last bit I was thinking of. Did you notice Luis's face as he gave me the news?'

Kate thought for a moment. 'Well, yes, now you come to mention it. He didn't look over-jubilant. Doesn't he get on with his brother?'

'Very well, all things considered.'

'How cryptic! Do I scent a mystery?'

Connie hesitated for a moment. 'There's no harm in telling you, I suppose. I mean it isn't as if it isn't common knowledge——'

'What is?' interrupted Kate. 'Come on, you can't leave it like that. You've whetted my appetite.'

'Well,' began Connie slowly, 'haven't you wondered why a man like Luis Antonio Vasconcelos, head of the Minvasco company, aristocratic, wealthy, not to mention attractive, happens to be unmarried?'

'No,' said Kate with misgiving. 'I'm afraid I haven't given it any thought at all. But I suppose it is rather odd.' She bit her lip. 'You're not going to tell me some dark, horrible secret I ought not to know, are you, Connie?'

The older woman looked taken aback. 'Whatever do you mean, Kate?'

'Well, he's—he's not gay, is he?'

Connie looked thunderstruck. 'Love a duck, Kate, of course he's not! Whatever gave you that idea?'

Kate looked embarrassed. 'Nothing, nothing. Pax, Connie. It was your mysterious hints, that's all.'

Connie needed more tea before her ruffled feathers were smoothed down sufficiently to tell a story which Kate listened to uneasily, as though she were trespassing on private property. Luis Vasconcelos, it seemed, had been betrothed from childhood to the daughter of a wealthy local landowner, a close friend of his parents. Once they arrived at a suitable age Luis and Pascoa Ribeiro were to be married.

'Pascoa!' said Kate swiftly.

'Yes, dear. Pascoa.' Connie sighed. 'Such a beautiful girl, with a nature to match. Sweet, devout, accomplished, everything any man could want in a wife. I suppose Luis had been so used to thinking of her as his future wife that he didn't really pay enough attention to her. Certainly not enough to see it was César she really cared for. Never could understand why myself. I mean, Luis and Claudio are handsome men by any standards, but César is quite ordinary. He's not as tall as the others, nor as good-looking—though,' added Connie judicially, 'he's very clever and ever so nice and kind. He's got a lovely nature.'

'So what happened?'

César, unable to bear the idea of Pascoa's marriage to Luis, persuaded his father to let him take charge of the vines and coffee in Parana, far away from Vila Nova. After he'd been gone a time it was noticed that Pascoa was unwell. She became listless and withdrawn, with no interest in her approaching wedding, nor in anything else. Luis, busy with the new responsibilities given him by his father in helping to run the head office of Minvasco in Vila Real, failed to notice the change in his *noiva* until it was too late.

'His *noiva*,' said Kate, nodding.

'Yes, love. That's fiancée in Portuguese.'

'It's one of the few words I know, as a matter of fact, but go on with your story.'

The mother of the prospective bride, never suspecting the real cause of her daughter's malaise for a moment, decided a stay with her sister in Rio de Janeiro would do Pascoa a world of good.

'So off she went,' said Connie. 'Her parents saw her off on the plane to Rio, but when she got there Pascoa rang her aunt to say she wasn't coming, then caught another plane to Santa Caterina and went straight to the *fazenda* in Parana where she stayed for a whole week with César before her parents, or anyone else, found out.'

'Bad news for Luis!'

'Exactly. There was a wedding right enough, but with César for bridegroom instead of Luis.'

Kate pulled a face. 'Don't tell me Luis was noble enough to be best man!'

'Lord, no, love. He took off to England well before and stayed away for a whole year. His father's illness brought him home in the end. A few weeks after he got back his dad was dead and Luis was the new *Patrão*.'

'And he's never shown signs of wanting to marry since?'

'No. Of course,' added Connie, suddenly rather pink. 'He's no monk, or anything. I mean——'

'No need to spell it out, Connie dear!' Kate looked thoughtful. 'He was in Parana just recently, though, wasn't he?'

'Oh, yes. It's all very civilised between him and César and Pascoa, and of course because he's the boss and all that Luis needs to visit Parana pretty regularly anyway. This time, though, he took his mum down because Pascoa was expecting her third baby.' Connie smiled. 'Good thing he did, too. Heaven help young Claudio if Dona Francisca finds out about his latest exploit!'

No wonder, thought Kate, that Luis Vasconcelos had it in for fiancées who forgot which man they were actually engaged to. A bit melodramatic, perhaps, but understandable.

To Kate's annoyance she woke very early next morning.

'I thought you'd be having a lie-in,' said Connie, when she found Kate up before her.

'So did I,' said Kate sheepishly. 'Maddening, isn't it? I fully intended lazing in bed for an extra hour, but I woke up at the crack of dawn, excited like a little kid over going out for the day!'

Connie laughed, and pressed Kate to a larger breakfast than usual, then took over the kitchen to stuff refrigerated bags with every conceivable cold delicacy, plus a wicker hamper she packed with silver and plates and Thermos flasks of soup and coffee in case the day turned chilly.

'Chilly!' said Kate, as she fetched and carried. 'But it's a gorgeous day.'

'It can be quite cold on these mountain roads, especially if we run into some mist. I thought we might go to Congonhos de Campo.'

Kate was quite happy to go anywhere Connie suggested, glad of the break after days of hard work at the Escola Francisca, as the new school was to be called.

'Unless Tony has a better idea,' said Connie, when everything was ready.

'Tony will fall in with whatever *we* decide,' said Kate with a grin.

Ten minutes later, arrayed in black trousers, white shirt and scarlet windbreaker, black leather brogues on her feet, her hair in her favourite corn-dolly plait tied with scarlet ribbon, Kate went out to throw a ball for Bruno until the car arrived. She was flushed and panting with exertion by the time the Mercedes drew up outside the double gates. With a final pat for the inexhaustible Bruno she ran to greet Tony, then halted in surprise as she found Luis Vasconcelos at the wheel instead of Dinis.

'Hi, Tony; good morning Senhor Vasconcelos,' she said breathlessly. 'What's happened to Dinis?'

'A family crisis, Miss Ashley,' said Luis, as he got out. He eyed her warily. 'I trust it will not spoil your day if I act as your driver for the *passeio* instead.'

Kate found she didn't object in the slightest. 'Of course not,' she assured him with a sunny smile which brought a look of relief to Tony's face.

'Pretty sporting, I thought,' he said quickly. 'To give up a whole day to us, I mean.'

'*De nada*, it is my pleasure,' Luis assured him. 'Perhaps you will allow me to give you lunch somewhere.'

Kate laughed. 'No need. All we want it some muscle to manhandle Connie's picnic baskets into the car. She's got enough food in there for an army!'

The outing went well from the start. Connie, utterly delighted to see Luis, insisted on taking a back seat with Tony while Kate sat in front to enjoy the view as they left Vila Nova behind and took a serpentine road which coiled itself through a breathtaking landscape of mountain peaks.

Kate was so taken up with the scenery that she quite forgot any constraint she might have felt in company with Luis Vasconcelos as he drove the car with skill along a road which edged precariously round one hill after another, with vertiginous drops at every turn, sometimes on both sides of the dusty red road connecting one peak to another.

'Now this is what I *call* a scenic route,' she said happily to Luis, who was dressed in much the same way as the night before, this time his sweater and cords a tawny brown, not unlike his eyes.

Tony, dressed as usual in denims, cotton shirt and navy sweater, plus a much-worn leather flying jacket and battered desert boots in honour of the occasion, was fascinated by the little roadside shrines they passed, most of them no more than a handful of flowers attached to a handmade wooden cross. 'That must be the fifth we've passed so far,' he remarked. 'What's the reason for them, Luis?'

Luis? thought Kate. That's new.

Luis explained that they marked the spot where some motorist had hurtled from the road to death, as was unfortunately so often the case.

'Really?' said Kate. 'Why so many?'

Luis shrugged. 'In part it is because many drivers have no money to spare for the maintenance of their vehicles. But the main reason is one of philosophy. The Arab, as you know, believes in Kismet, that Allah, or God, has written his fate from the time of his birth. Here in my country all believe that God *is* a Brazilian, and therefore will not allow any accident to happen.' He shot a look at Kate's startled face, laughing as he began to slow down. 'The road widens here. It is a good place to stop for our picnic lunch, *não é*, Connie?'

Luis manoeuvred the car into a natural niche in the rock edging the hillside, well away from the virtually non-existent traffic. Their vantage-point gave them a bird's eye view of the dusty red road which curled away into the distance around mountain ridges marching towards the horizon under a blazing blue sky.

There was a holiday atmosphere about the occasion as they feasted on hot, savoury soup and home-made rolls, pieces of cold chicken eaten with fat red tomatoes, and afterwards wedges of Connie's wonderfully British fruitcake, the meal washed down with fragrant hot coffee.

'*Obrigad*', Connie. *Maravilhoso,*' said Luis, as he sat on a tartan rug with his back against the rock, his face raised to the sun.

'I'm sorry your Dinis had a family problem,' said Connie, 'but I must say I'm glad you're here in his place just the same, Luis.'

'*Eu também,*' he answered lazily, eyes closed. '*Disculpe-me*, Miss Ashley. I said "I also".'

Tony lay flat on his back, utterly relaxed, his hands clasped behind his head. 'So say all of us,' he said, yawning. 'Sorry. I fall asleep here at the drop of a hat. Must be this air.'

Kate looked down at him, shaking her head. 'He does this every lunchtime, you know. Eats like a horse, then bingo, he's out like a light until I prod him awake for the afternoon session.'

'Sign of an untroubled conscience,' muttered Tony drowsily.

'I must have a lot on mine, then,' she said, sighing. 'I never even sleep the night through, let alone catnap in the day.'

'You will,' said Connie comfortably, 'once you get acclimatised. Who's for more coffee?'

A soft snore was Tony's only response.

Luis's eyes danced as he held out his beaker. '*Requiescat in pace,*' he whispered, winning a smothered giggle from Kate.

'I wonder if you'd mind if I sat in the car and had forty winks too?' said Connie, yawning. 'Tony's complaint is catching.'

'Of course not,' said Kate. 'I'll pack the baskets.'

Once Connie was installed comfortably with a cushion and a rug on the back seat of the car Luis returned to let himself down beside Kate. He waved a hand at the vista before them. 'So. Tell me what you think of *minha terra*, Miss Ashley—my homeland, you understand, this part of Minas Gerais where I was born.' He spoke very quietly, close to Kate's ear so that Tony could sleep undisturbed, and she sat very still, paralysed by a sudden attack of shyness.

She stared dumbly at the scene before her for a moment. 'It's rugged, with a sort of primitive grandeur,' she said slowly at last in an undertone, 'a picture painted in basic colours—vermilion, burnt Sienna, cobalt blue. An artist could only use oils to reproduce your country faithfully, Senhor Vasconcelos.'

He nodded in agreement. 'You are observant. You have an eye for such things. But I beg you will dispense with such formality. Could I not be simply Luis, and beg the privilege of your first name in return?'

Kate turned to look at him, her cheeks colouring as she found his face very near her own. She looked away hastily, staring straight ahead. 'If you wish,' she said rather stiffly. 'Though not in front of my pupils, please. It might undermine my authority.'

'I do not think so. Are you not known to them as Miss Kate?'

'Well, yes.'

'While your friend is just plain Tony to them, *não é?*'

'Ah, but he's a man, remember. It's different for him.'

'*Pois é.* But even though you are so very obviously a woman, I am sure you have no problems with the discipline.'

Kate shook her head. 'None. But then, I think you made very sure of that by coming along in person on the first day. Would you have bothered to do that if Phil Holmes had come instead of me, as originally intended?'

He shrugged. '*Quem sabe?* But since it was you who came, Kate, I wished to make it very clear that any man causing you trouble would answer to me.' Something in his voice, quiet though it was, made it very clear that the consequences of any familiarity would have been unpleasant in the extreme.

'Thank you. Everyone's been very polite and respectful, I assure you. On the other hand Tony's made it pretty plain *he* wouldn't put up with any nonsense on my behalf either.' Kate gave him a small, sidelong smile. 'I think I'm pretty well protected from all comers, between Connie, Tony—and you.'

'And you, Luis,' he prompted with a smile.

'And you, Luis,' she repeated obediently, then jumped to her feet. 'Time I cleared away, I think.'

'I shall help.' And, despite the fact that he was obviously a stranger to the task, Luis proved surprisingly efficient as he helped Kate pack the plates and leftovers away.

Tony sat up, yawning and rubbing his eyes, as Luis was stowing the last of the hampers in the boot. 'Can I do anything?' he asked as he scrambled to his feet.

'Now he asks!' said Kate scathingly, as she opened the car door. 'Connie,' she said gently. 'Wakey, wakey. Time to go.'

The blue eyes opened with suspicious ease, no trace of sleepiness in them as Connie sat up, smiling, patting her immaculate hair. 'Are we off, then, love?'

The claim to fame of the quiet little town of Congonhas de Campo was the sanctuary of Bom Jesus dos Matosinhos, the visitors were told, as Luis led them towards a church whose approach was lined with chapels containing over sixty lifesize figures carved in wood to represent the various stages of Christ's passion. Kate gazed at them in awe as Luis told them a little about the sculptor, Antonio Francisco Lisboa, known down the centuries as *O Aleijadinho*, 'The Little Cripple', because of the leprosy which disfigured his hands and face.

'Towards the end,' said Luis, 'his favourite slave Mauricio is said to have tied the—what is *formao*, Tony?'

'Chisel.'

'Ah, *sim*. The chisel was tied to the stumps of his hands for him to finish the miracles he created here.'

Kate wandered very slowly past the figures, amazed at the torment and suffering their creator had managed to carve into the wood. Further on she found that the sculptor had been equally skilled with stone. Twelve larger-than-life soapstone figures of the prophets stood sentinel on the terraced forecourt of the church.

Connie gave a little shiver as she pointed out the figure of Hosea. 'Look at the twisted legs. I remember José telling me it's supposed to be just like *Aleijadinho's* own deformity.'

'Poor guy,' said Tony with a shiver. 'But what an artist!'

'Yet so few people outside Brazil know of him,' said Luis, as they made their way back to the car. 'And even here, where he wrought his miracles, far too few visitors come to appreciate his genius.' He looked at Kate's subdued face and became brisk.

'Now, I think we have enough of the sightseeing for today.'

Kate was quiet on the return journey, letting Tony and Connie do most of the talking as Luis drove towards sunset along the winding red road.

'You have enjoyed the day, Kate?' asked Luis quietly, under cover of the animated conversation coming from the back.

'Very much indeed. Thank you.' She smiled at him. 'It was very good of you to take over for Dinis. Weren't there any other drivers free?'

He shrugged, keeping his eyes on the road. 'I did not enquire. I wished to come myself. I do not take as much time off as I should. I saw the beauties of my own country with new eyes today, in your company.' He gave her a quick, sidelong glance. 'Why? Would you have preferred someone else?'

'Of course not.'

'If Claudio had been given his way *he* would have come.'

'Is he well enough?' said Kate, surprised.

'He is recovered, yes, but there was no question of allowing him to accompany you on your day out.' He frowned suddenly. 'Nevertheless there is something I have been meaning to tell you, Kate——'

'Luis,' interrupted Connie, leaning forward. 'Tony's coming to dinner with us tonight. Won't you join us?'

'Alas, no, Connie. Tonight I must dine with some very boring gentlemen who will discuss only the price of coffee.' Luis threw a swift smile over his shoulder. 'Perhaps you will invite me some other evening.'

After which the conversation became general and it was only later, when Kate was in bed, that she remembered the unfinished sentence and wondered what Luis had intended to say.

She found out first thing the following Monday morning. After the memorable Saturday outing and a very peaceful, lazy Sunday doing almost nothing at all, Kate felt rested and full of enthusiasm for the day ahead when she arrived at the school with Tony.

But when she walked into the classroom her heart gave a sickening thump at the sight of a strange face among the group of young men. The face was not entirely strange to her. She'd seen it once before, when its owner fell at her feet unconscious and bleeding, in her hotel room in the Pouso da Rainha.

Kate faltered for an instant, almost stepping on Tony's foot as he followed behind.

'What's up?' he whispered.

'We have a new pupil.' Kate marched up to the podium, gazed down on the men assembled before her, and said a smiling 'hello' as usual.

There was a concerted 'hello' in response, then her star pupil, a bright young man by the name of Jaime da Silva, stepped forward to introduce the new addition to the class. Demonstrating his excellent recall of the session spent on manners, he presented the slim, handsome youth to Kate with much formality.

'How do you do, Mr Vasconcelos?' said Kate, not daring to look in Tony's direction. 'Welcome to the class.'

'*Muito prazer, Senhorita Ashley,*' responded Claudio, his eyes gleaming as he tried to raise her hand to his lips.

Kate withdrew her hand sharply. 'We speak only English here, Mr Vasconcelos.' She held out her hand again, and when he took it, bewildered, she shook hands briefly and moved back to the podium, informing the class that in Britain it was not the custom to kiss hands by way of greeting.

From the first the class had been divided into two groups which Kate and Tony took separately, alternating them morning and afternoon. After exchanging a look with Kate, Tony took Claudio to work with his own group in the next room, giving her time to recover from the rather nasty little surprise as she handed out the work she'd prepared over the weekend.

The first session was halfway through when the caretaker knocked at the door and said there was a telephone call for Kate. Excusing herself from her students, Kate hurried to the staff-room to pick up the telephone, not at all surprised to hear the voice of Luis Vasconcelos.

'Miss Ashley? Kate? Good morning. I trust you are well.'

'Good morning. I'm very well, thank you.'

'But angry, I think!'

'Not in the least,' lied Kate.

'Forgive me. Saturday was such a happy day that I did not wish to spoil it by telling you that Claudio would be joining your class today. I made one attempt, but was interrupted.' The husky, distinctive voice sounded sincerely regretful.

'It doesn't matter,' Kate assured him. 'I'm here to teach as many people as you like, Senhor Vasconcelos.'

'Ah! I am no longer Luis.'

'Certainly not here,' she reminded him tartly.

He sighed. 'I should have made it clear that Claudio was always intended to be one of your students. He was prevented from starting with the others due to circumstances which are regrettably well known to you.'

'They are indeed,' agreed Kate. 'He's destined for the London office, then?'

'Yes. César and I think it wise to remove him from here for a while. My mother disagrees of course, but, since it is I who is *Patrão*, the decision is mine to make.'

'Tony and I will both do our best to see he speaks a fair bit of English by the time we leave.'

'He already speaks a little. But ignore him if he tries to—to——'

'Show off?'

'Like a naughty child? *Exactamente*. If he annoys you in any way, do not hesitate to inform me. I will see that he causes you no further distress.'

'Don't worry, he won't,' Kate promised.

'He may try. He is accustomed to foolish behaviour from women because of that beautiful face of his, you understand.'

Kate grinned evilly. 'Not this woman! But, oddly enough, if Claudio does step out of line I fancy it's not only Tony who'll crack down on him, but the rest of the class, too. They actually seem to like us both, you know.'

'And who can blame them?' Luis riposted swiftly. 'To have a *professora* like you when I was a student would have seemed like a gift from heaven!'

Kate flushed, unseen. 'How extravagant. I must go. Thank you for ringing.'

'*De nada*. I shall be away in Sao Paulo until the end of the week. I shall check on my brother's progress when I return. *Adeus*, Kate.'

'*Bon voyage*.'

Kate felt much better as she put the phone down. An apology had by no means been necessary. As *Patrão* of Minvasco Luis Vasconcelos could put anyone he liked in her English class. Of course, Claudio was a special case, one way and another— brother of the *Patrão*, spectacularly handsome, convinced he was irresistible to all members of the opposite sex. Kate's lips curved in a smug little smile. It would do him no end of good to find there was an exception to the rule. Besides, she thought suddenly, when it came to looks Luis appealed to her far more than Claudio. She bit her lip. That little discovery was best kept secret from Connie, or her charming landlady's matchmaking tendencies were likely to get out of hand.

CHAPTER SIX

LUIS'S fears about his young brother proved unfounded. Right from the first there was no trouble from Claudio, other than a slight propensity for gazing at Kate dreamily sometimes instead of getting on with his work. Claudio Vasconcelos was no slouch as a student, and, Kate soon realised, he was very popular with the others, despite his rather awkward position as younger brother of the *Patrão*.

'Could have been worse,' commented Tony after a few days. 'I was prepared for fireworks when we found the cuckoo in the nest.'

Kate nodded wearily as she packed her bag, ready to go home. 'Claudio's no bother in my class—except for his habit of staring at me now and then. What's he like with you?'

'Well, he doesn't moon about after me, love, that's for sure!' Tony grinned. 'Actually he's pretty bright. Of course he could speak some English already, but considering the others had a fortnight's start on him he's doing remarkably well.'

'His brother must have laid it on thick about not being a nuisance, I suppose.'

'And Luis strikes me as being a man you wouldn't care to cross. After that messy business with the chef I expect Claudio's toeing the line pretty carefully. Here, give me your bag, Kate, you look tired.'

'Thanks.' Kate made a face. 'It must be the strain of having Claudio in the class. I seem wearier this week than I was at first.' She looked out of the window. 'No sign of Dinis yet.'

They waited for ten minutes or so, chatting idly as they watched the men finish on the construction site for the day. Suddenly a car came speeding along the road to the school to come to a screaming halt in a cloud of red dust. Claudio jumped out and ran into the building, and after a knock on the staff-room door he put his black, curly head round it, eyes and teeth gleaming as he smiled apologetically.

'Com licença, Senhorita Ashley, Senhor Morton——'

'English, Claudio,' said Tony automatically.

Again the flashing smile. 'I am sorry. The Mercedes has the puncture. Dinis apologises he cannot come. I was in the—the office of my brother, so I shall drive you to the home of Dona Connie instead.'

Kate was not at all sure she wanted to be driven anywhere by Claudio Vasconcelos, but after a nudge from Tony she accepted gracefully and allowed Claudio to instal her in the back of the small Fiat with much ceremony. And, although he chattered in fractured English to Tony all the time, to Kate's relief he drove with care on the short distance to Casa Londres, steering his Fiat right through the open double gates and up to the veranda, much to Connie's delight.

'Claudio!' she exclaimed, running down the steps. 'Como vai?'

Claudio kissed her on both cheeks. 'I am well now, Dona Connie, but please! We must speak the English.' He gave a laughing glance at Kate and Tony. 'My teachers will punish me if not.'

Suddenly Bruno shot across the garden like a bullet, ready to defend his mistress, then went mad with delight at the sight of Claudio, who fought the dog off, roaring with laughter, looking suddenly like the young boy he really was under the sophistication he tried so hard to maintain.

'You'll be back in hospital if you don't watch it,' said Tony, and pulled the dog away as Connie insisted they all had tea and some of her newly baked scones.

'But coffee for Claudio, of course,' she said, patting his arm as she went to call Elsa.

'You spoil me, Dona Connie,' he called after her.

'Doesn't everyone?' asked Kate, addressing a remark to him directly for the first time as she sat down in one of the wicker chairs.

Claudio looked suddenly sober. 'No, Miss Kate. My father did not. Luis does not, also.' Colour rose under his flawless olive skin. 'I was pleased to drive you home today, because I desire much to apologise to you for—for the shock and distress I caused you for being intruder in your room at the Pouso da Rainha.'

Kate shrugged, smiling faintly. 'Thank you. I accept the apology. After all, you didn't know who was in the room when you knocked on the door.'

He grimaced. 'I think—thought I was dying.'

Tony grinned. 'Kate thought so too. You frightened the life out of her.'

Claudio hung his head. 'I was big fool. Forgive me, Miss Kate.'

'Let's forget about it,' said Kate briskly, and smiled gratefully as Connie filled her teacup. 'Thanks, Connie, my throat's dry as a bone after shouting all day.'

'You have a pretty voice,' Claudio informed her fervently.

'Now don't you start any of your nonsense with Kate,' Connie warned him.

'It is not nonsense!' He looked wounded, then shrugged despondently. 'Besides, Luis tell me I must—must——'

'Behave yourself where Kate's concerned,' offered Connie, and passed the plate of scones to him. 'Here, have one of these, love.'

It was a pleasant little tea-party, and Claudio on his best behaviour was a very beguiling young man. Kate found it very easy to see how attractive he must be to most girls, though for her own part all she could feel was indulgence.

'Probably because he's so young,' she told Connie over dinner.

'Not all that much younger than you, Kate.'

Kate chuckled. 'No, I suppose you're right. But all I feel towards Claudio—though he wouldn't like it if he knew—is vaguely maternal. But then I feel like that towards Tony most of the time, too, and he's a year older than me.'

'How about Luis?'

'What about Luis?'

Connie poured cream on Kate's compote of figs with a lavish hand. 'Don't prevaricate. Do you feel motherly towards him, too?'

Kate paused. 'No,' she said at last.

'What *do* you feel, then?'

'I hardly know him, Connie.' Suddenly Kate's eyes sparkled in her narrow, tanned face. 'But I should think the only woman likely to feel motherly towards a man like Luis Vasconcelos is Dona Francisca!'

* * *

The days passed with surprising speed as the English class grew more proficient, progressing to written homework which gave Kate and Tony more to do themselves in the evenings. Tony took to dropping off at Casa Londres most days for tea, afterwards working for a couple of hours with Kate on preparation for next day's sessions before going off to the hotel for his dinner, or sometimes staying to eat the meal with Connie and Kate. By way of appreciation for Connie's kindness the following Saturday he invited both ladies to the Pouso da Rainha for dinner, an evening Kate enjoyed more than expected, since the deferential treatment received from Senhor Pedroso and all the staff indicated very plainly that the young English *professora* was held in general respect, despite the unfortunate incident during her brief stay at the hotel. Tony, it was plain to see, was a great favourite at the Pouso da Rainha, treated by everyone as an honorary Brazilian.

Kate would not admit, even to herself, that she was disappointed because there had been no word from Luis as promised. She decided he'd heard Claudio was getting on well and saw no reason to check with her personally on his brother's progress after all. Yet, she thought forlornly, it was ten days since she'd seen him, and there was no getting away from the fact that she would quite like to see him again. Which, of course, was a bit stupid whichever way one looked at it. Since he was so stringent on preserving her reputation he was unlikely to risk damage to it by paying any attention to her—even if he was so inclined. Which was doubtful. And even if he were she would be very foolish to take any notice. She was here to do a job, and at the end of it she would go home and never set eyes on Luis Vasconcelos again.

Kate threw herself into the teaching sessions with renewed vigour, with the idea of ridding her mind of any half-baked, nebulous yearnings towards a man like Luis. As the weekend approached she noticed signs of much animation among her class, and on enquiring the reason for it learned that they were wondering if Miss Kate would be attending the *festa* in the town at the weekend.

'It is the Festa de São João, Miss Kate,' Jaime da Silva informed her, his eyes shining. 'The people wear peasant dress and there are fires and *foguetes*—fireworks,' he added, 'and there is music and dancing in the street.'

'Sounds fun,' said Kate to Tony over lunch.

'I remember São João—midsummer fires and all that. He's rather a jolly, homespun sort of saint in this part of the world.' Tony grinned. 'It can get a bit rough sometimes. People tend to throw balloons full of flour and soot at each other.'

Kate pulled a face. 'A bit hard on the clothes, isn't it?'

'They get done up in costume—straw hats, flapping cotton shirts and trousers and the girls in shawls and full skirts, I think. My parents took me when I was a nipper, and I loved it. Probably because I was allowed to stay up late.'

Next day Claudio remained behind when the day's sessions were over, looking young and eager as a puppy as he begged Kate and Tony to join him with some of the others when they went into town on the Saturday evening to the *festa*.

'It will be much fun, Miss Kate,' he said with enthusiasm. 'Jaime brings his sister and Helio Nunes his sister also.'

Kate, who would once have said yes without a thought, eyed him warily. 'Older sisters?'

'It does not matter, Miss Kate.' Claudio looked eager. 'It is permitted for you, I swear.'

Tony interrupted swiftly in Portuguese to make sure Claudio clearly understood Kate's misgivings, and asked whether his brother would approve, something Tony rather glossed over when translating to Kate to say it would be perfectly acceptable for the *professora Inglêsa* to attend the festivities in a crowd of other people, as long as some of the other people were respectable females.

'I don't want to step on any toes,' said Kate doubtfully, very much aware that the toes in question belonged to Luis. 'We'll ask Dona Connie first,' she said to Claudio. 'If she says yes I'll come.'

His eyes lit up. 'I will tell the others,' he said, and hurried to join his friends, who were outside the door, waiting anxiously for Kate's answer.

'I heard you mention Luis, Tony,' said Kate. 'Were you asking if he'd approve?'

'Yes. Apparently he's still on his travels, anyway.'

Immediately Kate felt so much better now she knew the reason for Luis's silence that she decided it would be foolish to pass up the chance of soaking up some of the local colour at a real Brazilian *festa*.

'What do you think, Connie?' she asked later.

Connie saw no objection at all. 'It's very much a family sort of affair. There'll be people of all ages, and as long as you're in a mixed group you'll be fine, love. You go off and enjoy yourself. You must get fed up, staying in with me night after night.'

Although Kate denied this instantly, there was some truth in what Connie said. Some nights, when the stars hung low in the sky, Kate felt restless as she stared at them from her bedroom window, and wanted quite badly to go out with someone somewhere. It seemed such a waste of a romantic setting never to have male company to enjoy it with. Yet if she was completely honest the only male company she had any desire for was that of Luis Vasconcelos—and he seemed far too wrapped up in his business affairs to spare a thought for a lonely English girl left to her own devices every night.

After leading a quiet, uneventful social life since her arrival Kate felt rather excited as she got ready for her night out in Vila Nova, her anticipation heightened by the crackling sound of distant fireworks as the town prepared to celebrate the *festa*.

'They're supposed to be waking up São João,' explained Connie as Kate ran to the *sala* to show herself off.

'How do I look?' she said, twirling round.

'A proper picture, love.' Connie clapped her hands at the sight of Kate in a skirt once worn by her own Linda. Yards of swirling black cotton printed with enormous red poppies were cinched in at the waist by a wide black belt over one of Kate's own white cotton shirts, with a shawl borrowed from Connie for warmth. The sweep of fine black wool had sparkling bead embroidery which struck answering sparks from Kate's eyes as she did a little dance round the room in her flat-heeled black leather boots, showing a froth of white petticoat. Her hair, washed and brushed until it gleamed like satin, hung down over her shoulders from two tortoiseshell combs above ears sporting outsize gilt hoops.

'I'll probably lose all my credibility with my class if the lads see me like this,' said Kate ruefully, as she sat down to dinner.

'Not a bit of it. Tonight's a holiday, nothing to do with everyday life. Everyone goes out to enjoy themselves. You go on and do the same,' advised Connie cheerfully.

They had barely finished coffee when a burst of barking from Bruno heralded the arrival of the escort party and Tony ran up the steps with not only Claudio in attendance, but also Jaime da Silva, Helio Nunes and two pretty dark girls of her own age who could only be the sisters promised as suitable company for the evening. With much ceremony Claudio presented his colleagues and their sisters, Ana and Florinda, to Connie, and asked her permission very formally to escort Kate to the *festa*.

'May I leave the car here, Dona Connie?' he asked. 'There will be no place for it in town tonight.'

'Of course, dear—off you go. And Tony, mind you keep an eye on Kate.'

Claudio looked injured. 'I also shall protect Miss Kate.'

Connie looked unconvinced. 'You can both look after her—don't let her out of your sight!'

Kate felt a surge of excitement as she hurried with the others towards the centre of the town, where the glow from the bonfires lit up the night sky. It made no difference that she spoke very little Portuguese or the two girls virtually no English; they were joined by a common exhilaration as they reached the steep streets of the town centre. Tony took Kate's hand in an iron grip as they joined the crowds who danced and sang and jostled each other in the roped off areas, and with Claudio holding the other hand Kate joined in the dancing and singing with everyone else in the firelight to a background of crackling fireworks.

At one stage they stopped to watch a mock marriage performed in one of the tree-lined squares, complete with drunken 'priests' and an irate father holding a shotgun to the grinning groom's back, and Kate laughed and clapped her hands with the rest, then Claudio dragged her off into the dancing crowd, separating her from Tony. For a moment she felt a rush of panic until she glimpsed Tony's fair head above the crowd as he danced with Ana. Minutes later Claudio was wrenched away by a pretty dark girl who was soon forced to yield him to another and all at once Kate found herself alone in a sea of laughing, unfamiliar faces, her hand grabbed by a total stranger who tried to pull her into the dance. The man took no offence when she shook her head, smiling. He went off happily with another girl and Kate, growing more apprehensive by the minute, secured the shawl over her head and pushed her way through the crowd, craning her neck for sight of a familiar face, but with no success.

Having visited Vila Nova itself only once, Kate had no idea how to head for Casa Londres. It was a couple of hours since she'd arrived in the town with the others, and since then they'd danced and jostled their way through several streets and squares. Now she was completely disorientated. No point in panicking, she told herself firmly, dodging and twisting to elude hands which stretched out in carefree invitation.

Eventually she found herself in a square which looked vaguely familiar. The buildings were illumined by the biggest bonfire of all, and with a thrill of relief Kate recognised the *edifício Minvasco* on the far side. She pushed her way through the crowd with renewed determination until she reached the familiar pillared doorway. If she stayed here in the shadows perhaps Tony might have the sense to come here looking for her. Pulling the shawl low over her forehead, Kate edged to the back of the mosaic paving to flatten herself against the great double doors of the building. She leaned against one of them with a sigh of relief, then gave a little screech of fright as it opened behind her and she fell backwards into the arms of the last man in the world she would have chosen to run into at that particular moment in time.

Luis Vasconcelos slammed the door shut as he released her. *'O que é isso, filinha?'* he asked as he switched on one of the lights, then stared, thunder-struck, as Kate slid the shawl from her hair.

'I'm afraid I don't speak Portuguese, *Senhor Patrão*,' she said, with a touch of defiance, wishing the marble floor would open up and swallow her.

'Kate!' He seized her by the elbows. *'Deus me livre*, what are you doing here alone on a night like this? Are you mad?'

'You're hurting me,' she said in a small voice, and Luis released her with a muttered curse. 'I wasn't alone until a moment ago. But I got separated from Claudio in the crowd——'

'Claudio!' His eyes glittered under brows which met together in a black bar above them. 'You are saying you were foolish enough to come here tonight with my idiot of a brother?'

Kate sighed, and pushed a hand through her hair, which had lost its combs somewhere en route. 'Not only Claudio, Luis. There's a crowd of us; Tony, Jaime da Silva and Helio Nunes and their sisters Ana and Florinda. I wasn't sure I should come, after all the protocol you keep on about, but Connie said it would be all right if I came with a group. So I did,' she finished lamely, her eyes falling from the angry glitter in his.

Unlike his partying countrymen outside in the square, Luis Vasconcelos was dressed in one of his formal dark business suits, though in rather less immaculate fashion than usual. His tie hung loose from his open shirt collar, and his jaw was darkly shadowed, a perfect match for the smudges of fatigue beneath eyes fixed on Kate with a look which had her fidgeting like a schoolgirl.

'May I ask why,' he asked with flaying precision, 'you are no longer with this group of so-called friends? What has brought you here alone and breathless—and very frightened, I think?'

'It's no big deal,' she said, clearing her throat. 'I got separated from the others in the crowd, that's all. I got swept along a street and into this square. This building was the only place I knew so I thought I'd wait here until Tony or one of the others found me.'

'And if they had not?' he asked very softly.

Kate shook back her hair defiantly. 'I don't suppose I'd have come to any harm.'

'Your hair, alone, attracts attention in this country of *morenas*, Kate.' He shrugged. 'I also do not believe any real harm would have come to you, but you might have become very frightened by the time your careless escorts finally discovered you, I think.'

Her eyes dropped. 'I'm quite capable of taking care of myself, you know.'

Luis shot the bolts on the great doors, then turned to her with an air of purpose. 'That is something I think I will put to the test. If you had remained outside, alone and unescorted, perhaps I should demonstrate what, *exactamente*, you were inviting, Kate.'

And before she had time to realise what he meant he pulled her into his arms and held her there, laughing down into her incensed face for a moment before he bent his head to kiss her. Kate struggled, but his embrace tightened fiercely as a sudden, mutual reaction to each other's touch licked them both with the same flame. Kate's emotions, heightened by her recent fears, took over completely. Her mouth opened to his with a gasp, and her body, instead of fighting to get away, melted against his in such unrestrained response that Luis made a strangled sound deep in his throat, and moulded her close against him. His mouth grew wild in its demand, his tongue importuning hers, then a shred of sanity returned to Kate and she stiffened and began to struggle. His arms fell away instantly as she jumped away, her face flaming as she put her hands up to her hair.

'You see?' Luis said huskily, his voice so unsteady that it was unrecognisable. He stood with arms folded across his chest, as if to control the breathing Kate could see was as laboured as her own as silence lengthened between them in the vast, shadowed hall in disturbing contrast to the noise outside in the *praça*.

'I—I tied Connie's shawl over my hair,' she said at last, dismayed to find her voice as hoarse and uneven as his.

'And that would have been all the protection necessary, you think!' Luis's eyes glittered scornfully, his olive-skinned face oddly colourless. 'If you had arrived outside a moment later the doors would have been locked against you.'

'I never expected them to be open,' she said, her eyes falling. 'I just had some idea of waiting in the shadows near the only place familiar to me.'

Luis put a hand under her chin and raised her face to his. 'I have come straight from the airport to pick up some papers on my way home. I told Dinis to leave the car at the back of the building then join his family at the *festa*, that I would drive myself home. It must have been the hand of God which guided me to open the main door for a moment to look out at São João's fire before I left.'

Kate tried to breathe evenly. 'I must have given you quite a shock, falling through the door like that.'

'*É verdade!*' He looked down into her resentful eyes questioningly. 'You are angry because I kissed you?'

'I didn't like being kissed to teach me some sort of lesson, certainly!'

The tawny eyes flamed, but this time as Luis reached for her Kate was ready for him and dodged away.

'You're the one who talks incessantly about protecting my reputation, Senhor Vasconcelos, but it seems to me that you're the greatest danger to it!'

The heat drained from his face, leaving it blank as he gave her a formal little bow. 'You are right. I am sorry, Kate. Please forgive me. I shall take you home instantly. Unless,' he added sardonically, 'you wish to return to the festivities.'

'No!' Kate gave a little shiver. 'I certainly do not.' She eyed him uncertainly. 'But what about Tony and

Claudio and the others? They're probably hunting high and low for me.'

'I cannot feel any concern about these so-called escorts of yours, Kate.' Luis switched off the light and led her across the hall into a corridor where no light was necessary other than the glow from outside. They walked along it in simmering silence towards a small door which led into a cobbled alley where the Mercedes lay waiting. 'If they are worried it is only what they deserve,' he said bitingly as he locked the door behind them.

Strange, thought Kate, how one kiss could alter everything. Relations between them, never entirely relaxed, seemed strained to breaking-point as Luis drove away from Vila Nova by a circuitous route which took them some distance out of their way to avoid the crowds.

'I regret the necessity to take such a long route to Dona Connie's,' remarked Luis stiffly at one point.

'Not at all,' responded Kate in kind. 'I'm only too grateful for the lift home.'

'Where did Claudio leave his car?'

'At Casa Londres. We walked into town earlier on.'

Luis said something very brief and bitter in his own tongue. Soon afterwards the quiet, suburban streets were left behind and Kate saw with surprise that she was on familiar territory as the angular shapes of the half-built school came into view, dimly outlined in the starlight. She eyed the aquiline thrust of Luis's profile apprehensively as he turned off on the unmade road leading to the kindergarten to drive over the rough ground intended for the play area until he reached a spot behind the building, well hidden from the road. Kate felt a trickle of fear run down her spine as he switched off the ignition and killed the lights.

'What are you doing?' she demanded. 'Why have you stopped here?'

Luis sat very still beside her, preserving a nerve-racking silence for several moments. 'I am no less human than Claudio, I find,' he said at last, his voice oddly rough. 'I cannot forget what you said, Kate.'

'What did I say?'

'That my kiss was meant to punish only.' He thrust a hand through his hair, then turned to her in the darkness, reaching blindly for her hand. 'I wished to teach you a lesson, *é verdade*, but the method I chose was one I desired so much I could no longer resist temptation when fate sent you into my arms tonight.'

Kate swallowed hard, her heart beating like a drum as she tried to free her hand. 'Luis——'

'No, Kate. Listen. I wished you to know that I have wanted badly to kiss you for—for a very long time.' He laughed softly. 'Our first meeting was disaster, *não é*? When I saw you standing there in your robe with a glass in your hand and your hair tumbling down in so wanton a way, I thought, *sem duvida*, that you were the famous Sofia.'

'You were pretty rotten to me the second time we met, too, when you knew exactly who I was,' Kate reminded him unsteadily.

'That was different. Then, of course, I knew you were the teacher. But I still believed that in some way you had become involved with Claudio as soon as you set foot in Vila Nova. Such sudden romances are not unusual in Claudio's experience, you understand.'

'They most definitely are in mine!' she said tartly, and again tried to pull away but his fingers tightened.

'*Calma, carinha.* Do not be frightened, I implore.' He moved nearer, his voice suddenly low and urgent. 'I know so very well that I should not have brought you here like this, alone in the darkness. But I am a mere man, Kate Ashley, and what man with blood in his veins could resist such temptation?'

Kate sat very still, engaged in a hectic private battle with herself. Now, she knew clearly, was the moment to storm at Luis, to tell him to take her home immediately, that he had no right to bring her here in the dark and tell her things which made her shake in her shoes. Then she caught sight of the stars, which were so much bigger and brighter here than in England, those same stars which had made her so restless on so many evenings for something, if she was honest, exactly like the situation she found herself in right now. Then it was too late. The stars were blotted out by Luis's broad shoulders as he took her in his arms, and any protest she might have made died before it was born as he began to kiss her with a slow, mounting tenderness which made her tremble so much that he tightened his embrace to hold her still as he moved his lips to her tightly closed lids, her cheeks, her earlobes, and Kate gasped as she felt his mouth on her throat and slid her arms round his neck to hold him closer still.

Her response acted like a match to kindling. Passion flared like the bonfires in the streets, had them gasping against each other's lips as his itinerant hands found the curves outlined by the thin cotton of her shirt. Kate ground her chattering teeth as his fingers teased tips which stood erect in response through their thin covering, and she buried her burning face against the thunder of his heartbeat as he laid his cheek against her tumbled hair.

'*Namorada,*' he whispered. 'Do not be afraid.'

Kate gave a stifled little sob of laughter. 'I'm not afraid, exactly, Luis, but I know perfectly well we shouldn't be alone here together like this. What would my students think now if they could see the *professora Inglêsa* behaving like—like a wanton?'

He put her away from him an inch or two, shaking her gently. 'I forbid you to use this word. I will kill any man who so much as suggests such a thing!'

'It's what you thought when you first saw me!' She gave a shaky little laugh.

'Do not keep torturing me with reminders of that terrible night, *querida*!' He put up a hand to smooth her hair. 'It was folly to bring you here like this. It is not my way to yield to such mad impulses.'

Kate detached herself from his grasp firmly and sat upright in her seat, trying to tidy herself in the leather-scented darkness. 'I should have made you drive away again immediately.'

'But you did not, Kate,' he said caressingly, and caught her hand in his to raise it to his lips.

Kate clenched teeth which tried to chatter again. 'No harm done,' she said cheerfully after a while. 'We were just caught up in the party atmosphere, that's all.'

His fingers closed like a vice on hers. 'Is that what you believe?'

She sighed. 'Shall we say it's what I'd better believe? We're two adult people, Luis Vasconcelos, who know very well that kisses like those just now tend to lead to a great deal more than just kissing. So I think you should know that I'm not in the market for—for a little holiday idyll with a man I'm never likely to see again once I return to England.'

Luis sat bolt upright in his seat. 'You mistake me, Kate Ashley! It is true that I brought you here tonight like some romantic idiot, but I had no thought of anything other than a kiss or two—if you permitted. If you had not I would have driven you straight home, *naturalmente.*'

'So it's my fault!' said Kate.

'For the kisses, no,' he said harshly, as he started the car. 'But to consider me guilty of such *grosseria* as seduction in a place like this, then yes, the fault is yours. I apologise for bringing you here... *meu Deus*, listen to me—I have made more apologies to you than to any woman in my entire life!'

The short journey to Casa Londres was accomplished in about half the time Dinis took each day. Kate hung on to her seat as Luis drive along the winding road with all the speed and panache of his countryman, Ayrton Senna.

'Where's the black and white flag?' enquired Kate acidly as he brought the car to a screaming halt in the road a little way from the house.

'Como?' Luis said blankly as he helped her out.

'My little joke. I just wondered if you were practising for the Brazilian Grand Prix.'

'You were in no danger,' he said stiffly.

'Less when you're at the wheel than when you're parked, perhaps!' she snapped, then stopped short in the drive of Casa Londres, which was ablaze with light from every window.

For once Kate had no attention to spare for Bruno's noisy welcome. With Luis close behind her she raced up the veranda steps to burst in on a scene of high drama in the *sala*. Connie, desperately pale and looking every year of her age, stood in the middle of the room trying to quieten two hysterical, sobbing girls.

'Connie!' said Kate, alarmed. 'What's the matter?'

For a split second Connie stared in disbelief, then she pushed the girls aside without ceremony and rushed to clasp Kate in her arms.

'Nothing's the matter now, darling!' she cried, her hand smoothing back Kate's hair. 'Oh, lord love us, Kate, whatever happened to you? We've all been going out of our minds! And Luis—wherever did you come from? I thought you were away.'

'I got separated from the rest and then—then I ran into Luis,' said Kate, stumbling over the last part as Ana and Florinda seized her hands and burst into an impassioned torrent of Portuguese, which Luis translated as desperate apologies until the flood dried up abruptly as the girls realised who he was and wilted into awed silence.

'Are you all right, Connie?' asked Luis urgently. 'You are very pale.'

'Pale?' Connie rallied bravely. 'I should think you'd be pale too if you'd thought Kate was out there lost somewhere.'

'I'm very sorry,' said Kate miserably. 'But there was such a crowd. One minute I was with Claudio, then suddenly I couldn't find anybody.'

Luis's eyes narrowed. 'Ah, yes, Claudio. Tell me, Connie, *por favor*, just exactly where *is* my young idiot of a brother?'

CHAPTER SEVEN

WHEN Claudio, Tony and the rest of the gang had arrived back at Casa Londres they had panicked when they found Kate had not, as hoped, found her way back there somehow. The men had immediately taken off again, Jaime and Helio on foot and Claudio with Tony in the Fiat, to search Vila Nova until Kate was found.

'I wanted to ring the police,' said Connie, 'but Tony thought Kate wouldn't like that, so I gave them until midnight, and if they weren't back by then I was going to contact the police anyway.' She frowned as she took in Kate's appearance properly for the first time. 'Goodness, child, you look as though you've been pulled through a hedge backwards. Go and tidy yourself up while I make some coffee for us all. Unless you'd like something stronger, Luis?'

Luis met Kate's eyes fleetingly before accepting Connie's offer gratefully. 'You permit that I wait here for Claudio, Connie, *por favor*?'

'Of course, dear.' Connie rounded up Ana and Florinda. 'I'll take these two off to help in the kitchen. Give them something to do.'

Kate was glad of a moment to herself in her room. One horrified look in the mirror had her reaching for a hairbrush and lipstick, shivering as she repaired the visible effects of Luis's lovemaking, uncertain whether she was cold or suffering from reaction.

When Kate returned to the *sala* she found it deserted, and Luis out on the veranda smoking a cigar. He turned at the rail as he saw her and beckoned her to join him.

'The glow in the sky is dying,' he remarked as she stood beside him. 'Soon São João may sleep for another year.'

'The party's over.'

'This one, yes. We have others.' Luis glanced sideways at her. 'Are we no longer friends, Kate?'

'I don't suppose we've known each other long enough to be friends, anyway,' she said rather sadly.

'Whereas it takes only a moment to become lovers.'

She looked up at him, startled. 'You said you had no intention of anything like that.'

Luis's teeth flashed white in the dim light. 'I was angry because you feared I would be so barbarous as to try to make love to you in a car. It would be *mentira*—a lie—to say I did not burn with the desire to do so, Kate.'

Her colour rose in a tide behind her tan, and he smiled, touching a fingertip to her hot cheek.

'You have a lover in England, Kate?'

She stiffened. 'No, I do not. I have friends who are men, just like I have others who are women. But I sleep alone.'

He studied her intently. 'How old are you, *carinha*?'

'Twenty-five.'

'Has no man ever asked you to marry him?'

'Yes. More than one, if we're counting.'

'Yet you are still *solteira*.'

'Yes.' Kate eyed him challengingly. 'So are you, if it comes to that.'

'Ah, but I fully expected to marry at one time.' He paused, looking down at her quickly averted face. 'Connie has told you that my *noiva* did not want me for a husband? That she preferred my brother?'

'Yes. I hope you don't mind.'

He shrugged. 'It is common knowledge to all in Vila Nova. It is also a very long time since I "minded", as you say.'

At a sudden clatter of cups they turned towards the *sala*, where Connie was overseeing Ana and Florinda as they brought in trays of coffee and sandwiches. She smiled at Kate and Luis cheerfully.

'That's better, love. You looked like something the cat dragged in when you got here. We've made some tea for you, and there's Scotch for Luis.'

Luis refused whisky in favour of coffee, pleading fatigue and the need to drive home if ever his young brother put in an appearance. He looked at his watch. 'It is late. I think I should go to look for him.'

'Nonsense,' said Connie firmly. 'You'd probably only miss each other.'

Kate did her best to put the girls at ease as she drank her tea, which was rather exhausting with the limited common vocabulary they shared, and it was a relief all round when a flurry of barking from Bruno, followed by the slamming of car doors, indicated that Claudio and Tony had returned.

'Go to your room for a moment, Kate,' ordered Luis abruptly.

'But——'

'Do as I say! Claudio must be taught a lesson.'

At an encouraging nod from Connie, Kate went from the room, but only as far as the hall, at a point where she could see part of the *sala*. She hugged her arms across her chest in distress as Claudio and Tony burst into the *sala*, both of them wild-eyed and distraught, their misery escalating at the sight of Luis, who stood tall and erect to confront them, the very personification of retribution. Claudio paled dramatically, his smooth olive skin suddenly transparent as his horrified eyes met the stern gaze of his brother.

'You have not found Miss Kate,' stated Luis in a bone-chilling voice.

'We've searched high and low,' groaned Tony in anguish. 'For Pete's sake call the police, Luis!'

Kate longed to put an end to Tony's misery then and there, but something about the set of Luis's shoulders decided her to remain hidden until he'd accomplished whatever it was he had in mind for Claudio.

'You were responsible for Miss Kate's safety, *não é*?' he asked his brother coldly.

Claudio nodded wretchedly. '*Eu sei, eu sei—é minha culpa——*'

'*Fala Inglês!*' Luis commanded.

'I do not know what happen, Luis. We are all dancing, Kate also.' He threw out his hands in despair. 'I was pulled away from her. I lost her. I found Tony. We searched. Jaime and Helio also. We brought Ana and Florinda here to see if Kate came back alone...' He gulped, blinking rapidly, all too plainly fighting against tears as Tony took over.

'Kate couldn't have been gone a minute or two, honestly. She seemed to vanish into thin air—but why the hell are we standing arguing here? If you won't call the police, I will!' And Tony brushed past Luis, his face grey with worry as he made for the telephone in the hall, his feet almost skidding on the polished floor as he found Kate standing there. He grabbed her by the elbows, shaking her violently. 'What the hell are you playing at, you little idiot? We've gone insane, looking for you——'

Luis tossed him aside, and led a remorseful Kate back into the *sala*.

'I asked her to remain hidden for a moment to teach Claudio—and possibly you, also, Tony—a lesson. You, of course, are not my responsibility, but this brother of mine *is*, *infelizmente*.' Luis turned a scathing look on the boy, as Claudio, the sight of Kate too much for him, gave way to the tears he'd been trying to hold back. Instantly Ana, Florinda and Connie converged on him to comfort him, the two girls leaping away in embarrassment at a curt command from Luis.

'I think it is time we left you in peace, Connie. I apologise on my brother's behalf for the worry and distress you have been caused.' Luis bowed very formally to Kate. 'To you also, Miss Kate, I tender my apologies for this evening.'

Kate shook her head. '*De nada*, as you say here. A storm in a teacup. I'm sure we'll all forget about it in the morning.' She moved over to Claudio and gave him an encouraging smile. 'Cheer up, Claudio. I came to no harm in the end.'

'That's right,' said Connie. 'All's well that ends well. Now it's time everyone went home to bed, I think. You must all be worn out, one way and another.'

Claudio, racked with shame over his tears and his lack of care towards Kate, bade her a subdued good-night coupled with another passionate apology, while

Tony, rigid with fury, ignored Kate very deliberately as he said goodnight to Connie, then went off with Claudio in the Fiat.

'I will drive the girls home, Connie,' announced Luis, then repeated it in Portuguese for the benefit of Ana and Florinda, who looked even more shattered than before at the prospect.

'I think they'd better wash their faces and tidy themselves up before they get back to their mothers,' said Connie, and took the girls off to the bathroom, leaving Kate and Luis alone.

'Did you have to be so perfectly bloody to Tony and Claudio?' Kate burst out in passionate resentment. 'You were cruel, Luis—utterly sadistic.'

'It is time Claudio learned a lesson once and for all,' said Luis and glanced towards the hall. 'Come. Let us go outside on the veranda.'

'No!' She dodged away, but Luis seized her by the arm and hauled her outside into the shadows at the end of the veranda, where he took her in his arms and kissed her with a hunger which shook Kate to the core.

Luis raised his head a fraction, breathing hard. 'I did not wish you to think my apologies were for the kisses also. I am *not* sorry I kissed you. And do not try to lie to me, because you are not sorry also. *Boa noite. Dorme bem.*' And with another swift, hard kiss on her parted lips he started down the veranda steps to quieten Bruno just as Jaime da Silva and Helio Nunes arrived, full of yet more apologies, as they came to collect their respective sisters.

'What a night!' said Connie, later, as she yawned with Kate over yet another pot of tea.

Kate smiled ruefully. 'Sorry to put the wind up you like that.'

Connie eyed her speculatively. 'It wasn't much fun at the time, but I'm a tough old bird. I'll survive. Though I think I qualify for the real story, miss. It seems ever such a coincidence that you lost Claudio only to find Luis.'

Kate flushed as she gave Connie an abridged version of the evening's events.

Connie, however, who was a very shrewd lady, seized immediately on a glaring discrepancy in the narrative. 'But if you got to Luis's place pretty quickly, what took you so long to come home? The boys were searching for ages.' Her eyebrows rose. 'Or is there something you're keeping from Auntie Connie?'

Kate munched on a chicken sandwich to give herself time. 'Luis had to take a very long way round in the car to skirt the crowds.' She met Connie's eyes, and shrugged, defeated. 'Oh, all right. He—er—he parked the car near the school so we could have a chat, that's all.'

Connie hooted. 'A chat! Pull the other one, dearie. I saw the state of you when you came in, remember! All right, I won't tease you any more, but if you ask me I think our Luis fancies you rotten, Kate. How about you? Do you fancy *him*?'

Kate opened her mouth to deny it, then changed her mind. What was the use? Connie's eyes never missed a thing. 'Yes,' she said sighing. 'I do. Once I got over the trauma of our first couple of encounters it didn't take long to see he's a very attractive man. But there's no future in *that* way of thinking, is there?

I'm here merely to do a job. I'll be gone soon, and that'll be that.'

'I came over here to do a job, too,' said Connie, with a faraway look in her eye. 'I got a nursing post at the Strangers' Hospital in Rio, you know. In those days you travelled by sea. It used to take seventeen days from London to Rio. José had been in England on some course Luis's father, the old *Patrão*, sent him on.'

'A real shipboard romance!'

'More than a romance, dear.' Connie grinned mischievously. 'I never did get to the Strangers' Hospital. José and I were married as soon as we got to dry land.'

'Good heavens—as quick as that?'

'I didn't half get a rollicking from my mum and dad. Called me every kind of idiot for marrying a foreigner—mind you, anyone born ten miles from Camberwell was a foreigner to them.' Connie looked Kate straight in the eye. 'What I'm trying to say, love, in my own inept way, is that nationality, religion, language—none of 'em makes a blind bit of difference when two people fall in love.'

Kate, deeply preoccupied with Connie's little pronouncement as she undressed, fully expected to lie awake all night, but to her horror it was almost eleven when she came to next morning. She shot out of bed to shower and dress at top speed, and arrived on the veranda to find Tony with Connie, unusually smart in an expensive Italian sweater and immaculately pressed grey trousers.

'Good morning, Connie,' Kate said breathlessly, 'sorry I'm late. Hello, Tony.'

'Morning, love,' said her hostess placidly. 'Have some coffee. Want something to eat?'

'No, thanks.' Kate eyed Tony warily. 'Sorry about last night.'

He got up to kiss her on the cheek. 'I should be apologising, not you. Sorry I went for you like that, but I was bloody frantic when there was no sign of you in the town. Then to find you hiding in the hall was the last straw. I could have throttled you with my bare hands.'

'I gathered that.' Kate shrugged. 'It wasn't my idea. Luis had some grim notion about teaching Claudio a lesson once and for all.'

'It was as much my fault as Claudio's!'

'I told Tony what really happened to you,' said Connie.

'Quite extraordinary luck that you ran into Luis,' remarked Tony thoughtfully.

'I panicked a bit when I got swept away in the crowd, so when I found myself near the Minvasco building it seemed a good idea to stay put there until you found me—which I knew you would sooner or later. It was pure chance that Luis happened to call in on his way home from the airport.' Kate poured herself more coffee. 'Now let's talk about something else, shall we? You're very elegant today. Going somewhere?'

'We're all going somewhere,' said Connie. 'Luis has asked us to lunch at Casa dos Sonhos to make up for last night.'

Kate's heart gave a sickening thump. 'No!' she said in a panic. 'I don't feel up to socialising. I've—I've got a headache after all the excitement. Would you give my thanks to Luis and make my apologies for me? I need a quiet day to recharge my batteries.'

Tony, surprised, did his best to dissuade her, but Connie remained oddly silent, her eyes troubled as they searched Kate's obdurate face.

'Are you sure, love?' she asked.

Kate smiled brightly. 'Absolutely, Connie.'

'Then come into the kitchen and let's see what we can find for your lunch.' As soon as they were alone Connie took Kate's hand. 'Are you staying home because of what happened last night, love?'

Kate nodded unhappily. 'Yes, Connie. I don't fancy toting a broken heart home among my luggage. So I'm being a good, sensible girl and keeping out of Luis's way.'

'Seems a pity,' said Connie, shaking her head. 'A definite waste, in fact. What shall I tell him?'

'That I've got a headache, just as I said.'

'He won't believe me.'

'Possibly not. But he'll get the message.'

Although Kate kept to her room when Claudio arrived to collect his brother's lunch guests she could hear his exclamations of regret all the way from the veranda. Once everyone had gone Kate sighed as Bruno settled back into a silence which soon penetrated the house and gave Kate doubts about her own sanity. What a fool she was in a way to pass up the chance of lunch with Luis at Casa dos Sonhos. Wistfully she pictured the house as it must look in the brilliant noon sunlight, of the delicious lunch they would eat in the rather grand, formal dining-room. And above all she kept thinking of Luis, and how he would react when he realised she'd deliberately stayed away. He was bound to take it as a personal affront, but at least he'd get the message without a face-to-face confrontation.

She shivered. It would be madness to risk more scenes like last night. So far she'd survived remarkably well without succumbing to the temptations of a physical relationship. But Luis Antonio Vasconcelos might well prove the one man in the world able to tempt her beyond all resistance, which would be fatal. How on earth would she ever get on with her life afterwards if she became Luis's lover for the brief time she was in Vila Nova? Not that there was much likelihood of that in this particular Brazilian backwater. The alternative, of meeting him in public without any opportunity for interludes like last night, was equally unappealing. One was hardly likely to expire from sexual frustration, reflected Kate bleakly. Nevertheless her first introduction to it the night before had been a salutary experience. It had horrified and amazed her to find that a few kisses were enough to leave her burning for a man to take his lovemaking to the ravishing conclusion she was certain it would be with Luis Vasconcelos.

These sensible conclusions proved bleak company as Kate struggled to lose herself in preparation for the following day's lessons. Later, after a sandwich lunch which Bruno shared with enthusiasm, Kate threw a ball for the eager dog in the back garden until her arm ached and she was glad to subside in one of the deckchairs kept in the small paved area which Connie refused to glorify with the description 'patio'.

The sun was very hot during early afternoon, even in the cold season. Kate abandoned her novel to lie with her face to the warmth, doing her best to keep her mind blank as she took advantage of her solitude to top up the tan which looked so good against her eyes and hair. Still tired from the night before she dozed a little at last, then woke feeling chilly to find Bruno fawning over a tall figure which stood between herself and the sun.

'Luis?' said Kate in astonishment, her heart hammering as she shot upright.

'A small Minvasco problem called me away from my guests,' he said without expression, as he bent to stroke the dog. 'Should you be lying in the sun with so severe a headache, Kate?'

She jumped to her feet, pushing a hand through hair embarrassingly untidy after her romp with Bruno. 'The headache was merely an excuse. I'm sure I don't need to explain why.'

'Are you saying that after—after last night you could not endure the sight of me today?' One of the straight black brows rose a little, but otherwise there was no spark of expression to indicate whether he was angry, or offended, or even amused.

Kate sighed. 'I kept away from you today because that's the way I mean to go on until I leave Vila Nova.' She bent to pick up her book to avoid the look in his eyes, which unsettled her badly. 'Last night...' She swallowed, then began again. 'Last night was an isolated incident which I'm sure you don't intend to repeat, anyway.'

'How can you think that?' he asked hotly. 'After holding you in my arms and feeling you respond to my kisses I would have to be made of stone not to desire such joy again.'

Kate forced herself to look him in the eye. 'Which is why I've decided to keep out of your way.'

'You found my kisses so distasteful?' he said harshly.

'*No!* That's the point. I didn't!' She flung away. 'But I'm only here for a short time. I can't let myself get involved.'

'Why not? Is there some sin in a relationship with a man? I came here today to ask you...' He halted tantalisingly, and Kate's heart leapt in her breast.

'To ask me what?' she whispered, her eyes wide in her tense face as she turned to him.

'I came to ask that we should be friends.' He gave a short, mirthless laugh. 'I had persuaded myself, you understand, that this would be possible. But now I see you again I know that it is not. I have no wish to be one of these men "friends" of yours. I wish, *Deus me ajuda*, to be your lover.'

'My lover!' she said scornfully, utterly mortified that she could have thought for a moment that he'd meant something very different.

'I cannot offer you any other relationship,' he said flatly. 'I long ago lost my belief in the fairy-tale of marriage. My father was not faithful to my mother. Pascoa deserted me for my brother. I do not believe it possible for one man and one woman to remain faithful to each other forever.' He shrugged. 'There is no law which says I must marry. The name Vasconcelos will go on with César's sons, no doubt Claudio's also, in time.'

Kate's chin rose. 'What's all that to do with me?'

He smiled suddenly, his eyes caressing. 'Do not pretend you do not understand, Kate. I know you must finish with the lessons, but once they are over let me take you away to Rio, to Acapulco, anywhere in the world you like. To be my *amante*, *querida*. Because once the London office is open I shall visit there often. I can buy you an apartment, or even a little house——'

'You're not serious!' said Kate incredulously. 'Are you actually asking me to be your *mistress*? No way!'

For answer he seized her in his arms, dragging her hard against him. '*Sim, querida*, I am deadly serious.' He kissed her fiercely, setting his hand flat against the base of her spine to hold her in close contact with the pulsing proof of his need of her. Heat washed over Kate's body in a relentless tide as he dealt impatiently with the buttons of her shirt, then pulled away the scrap of satin beneath. At the touch of his hot, seeking mouth on her bare skin, Kate let out a choked sound of denial and tried to push him away, but Luis swept her up off her feet against his chest, oblivious to her pummelling fists or the excited barking of the dog as he strode with her into the house.

Kate fought him every step of the way, frightened out of her wits as Luis ignored her, tossed her down on her bed and kept her there by the simple means of lying full length on top of her. Deaf to her hoarse entreaties, he held both her hands high above her head in one of his as he loosened her belt, his mouth moving, devouring, in a downward path which led unerringly to the irresistible lure of a taut crimson nipple. His lips closed on it hungrily, and Kate let out a low, shamed moan of helpless response as she made the chilling discovery that one medium-size girl, however fit she might be, was no match for a man not only taller, heavier, and in prime physical condition, but in the grip of sexual desire so strong that he meant to possess her whether she wanted it or not. She dredged up every last ounce of resistance and began to fight in deadly earnest until at last she freed one of her hands and made contact with the quartz ashtray Connie provided for guests who smoked.

Kate let herself go limp, convincing Luis for a second that victory was his. But even as he uttered a choked, gloating sound of triumph, she brought up her arm and crashed the quartz down against his temple.

Kate lay spreadeagled under the sudden dead weight of her would-be lover, terrified she'd killed him. But as she struggled away from him she found Luis merely stunned slightly, and, she realised in panic, utterly furious. Hastily she resumed her shirt, adding a sweater from the back of a chair for good measure and buckled her belt, her eyes glittering with rage as he rose slowly to his feet, his face set in harsh, carved lines.

'Perdoneme,' he ground out, manfully ignoring the fact that one eye was swelling already from contact with the ashtray. 'I regret my mistake. I had deluded myself that you wanted me as I want you.'

'Your choice of vocabulary is *so* apt!' Kate said bitingly. 'Delusion's the word if you think I'm the type to welcome a casual session in bed between your lunch party and a trip to the office!' She hugged herself hard against the hurt and distaste which shook her. 'Please go. Your guests must be wondering what's keeping you.'

He lifted one shoulder indifferently. 'They will not expect me yet. I have not been to my office. There was no emergency. I lied. I wished to see you alone again so that I could——'

'Enjoy a quick session in bed as dessert!' she said with scorn. 'You really got the wrong end of the stick last night, didn't you? *So* sorry, Senhor Vasconcelos. I'm not available for trips to Rio or wherever, nor to play house in some sordid little love-nest somewhere.'

'It is you who make it sordid!' He moved nearer, suddenly menacing, and Kate backed away, willing herself not to show fear.

'Possibly,' she snapped. 'But that's the way it sounded to me. If I could possibly do so I'd leave at once, but I can't. I'm contracted to the school to teach English to your employees, so I'll stay and finish the course. But——' she threw her head back challengingly, fiercely pleased to see that his eye was beginning to close '—during the short time left I would be grateful if you'd arrange it so that I never lay eyes on you again.'

'Is that truly what you desire?' Negligently he caught her in his arms and kissed her once, hard and emphatically, then stepped back. '*Engraçado*, because you are not indifferent to me, Kate. You lie if you deny it.'

She breathed in deeply, her eyes glittering with dislike. 'I do deny it. Goodbye, Luis.'

He shrugged, the indifference in his face sudden and insulting. '*Não faz mal*—no matter. It is never difficult to find beautiful ladies more accommodating than you.'

Kate clenched her teeth. 'I'm sure it isn't. Will you please *go*? I don't want the others to come back and find you here.'

'Perhaps I was mistaken,' he said musingly as he sauntered to the door. 'Last night, when you came to me lost and frightened and helpless, I felt something I had never felt before for a woman. I wished to protect you, to cherish you against any fear you might experience again. This was new to me, you understand. It misled me into feeling that what we could have together would be special, different.'

'Then why were you so brutal just now?' said Kate, his words shaking her badly.

'It was not my intention. But suddenly I wanted you so much I lost my head.' He looked oddly detached, as though he were discussing someone else. 'This never happened to me before. I must have been *louco*—mad—for a moment. Perhaps I believed that if we made love together it would persuade you to be my *amante—quem sabe*?' He gave her a twisted smile. '*Adeus*, little English teacher. I hope one day you find a man you want for a lover. Do not wait too long. Life is short, *não é*?' He came back to her and touched a slim brown finger to her cheek, then strode from the room, his footsteps brisk and assertive on the polished boards of Connie's veranda, reminding her all too vividly of their first encounter at the Pouso da Rainha.

CHAPTER EIGHT

THE English lessons proceeded at a spanking pace, with gratifying results. The seven students enjoyed working with the young English teachers, all of them eager to please Tony and Kate by becoming fluent in their language well before the end of the course.

Kate worked desperately hard, determined to show Luis Vasconcelos that her work was in no way affected by their bitter quarrel. Nevertheless, having told Luis she never wanted to set eyes on him again Kate found life with no prospect of doing so a very bleak affair. There was, she learned quite early on, no possibility of running into him by accident, since he was once more in Parana, where Pascoa Vasconcelos was taking such a long time to recover from the birth of her son that Dona Francisca felt obliged to remain. César, anxious to be with his wife as much as possible, had asked Luis to take over the reins for a while, leaving Julio Alves at the reins in Vila Nova.

'When I have the experience I shall take over here and Luis can stay in Parana always,' declared Claudio one day, as he waited to drive them home in place of Dinis, who was on holiday.

'Does he want that?' asked Tony, surprised.

Claudio shrugged. 'It is my opinion that he desires to be near Pascoa, you understand, no matter that she is César's wife.'

Kate busied herself with packing her bag to hide her reaction to this crushing piece of news.

'He should marry,' went on Claudio blithely. 'A man needs a woman of his own, *não é*?'

Tony laughed, then whistled as he glanced through the window. 'Talking of women, *amigo*, who's the gorgeous bird hanging about out there?'

Claudio swaggered to the window, then jumped back again in dismay. *'Nossa senhora—é Sofia!'*

'Sofia?' Kate rushed over to the window to see a girl fidgeting outside near the Fiat, casting nervous glances over her shoulder. Her hair flowed like black satin down to the neckline of a red dress which appeared glued to every line of her ripely curved body.

'Wow!' Tony grinned at Claudio over his shoulder. 'So that's the famous Sofia.'

Claudio's hand was clamped to his side, as if he felt the chef's blade all over again. He implored Tony to send her away, tell her he wasn't there, ill or dead, anything to make her go away and leave him alone. Terrified that the vengeful chef would kill him this time if the faithless Sofia was seen anywhere in his vicinity, Claudio finally persuaded Tony to go outside to talk to the girl.

Kate watched through the window, giving the nervous Claudio a running commentary as Tony greeted the girl with a polite smile, listening courteously as Sofia talked to him with much flirtatious eye-fluttering and gleaming of teeth.

'Not shy, is she?' said Kate, amused.

'Shy!' Claudio shuddered. 'She is man-eater! I was fool to be so *doido*—I mean mad for her, Miss Kate.'

'I get the drift.' She patted his hand soothingly. 'Anyway I think Tony's managed to convince her you aren't here.'

Very gingerly Claudio crept close enough to the window to watch the hip-swinging retreat of his erstwhile paramour as she walked away from the school, tossing back her hair in case Tony was watching her go. Which he was.

'OK, Claudio,' said Tony as he came back. 'All clear. She's on her way back into town.'

'Graças a Deus!' said the boy fervently as he wrung Tony's hand. *'Muito obrigad'*, Tony. I owe you one.' He gave a wicked grin at Kate. 'That is right, Miss Kate?'

'Absolutely!'

Claudio was so light-headed with relief on the short drive back to Casa Londres that he sang snatches of carnival songs to his companions, insisting they join in the chorus as he stopped the car with a squeal of brakes at the foot of the veranda steps. Their rowdy attempt at harmony died a quick death when they realised that Connie was not alone.

Luis Vasconcelos rose to his feet, his face darkly tanned, marks of fatigue under his eyes as he held out his hand to Kate.

'Boa tarde, Miss Kate. Are you well?'

Up to that moment Kate had been confident that she was perfectly fine, well on the way to recovery from the trauma of her brief acquaintance with Luis Vasconcelos. A single glance at his unsmiling face was enough to put paid to that idea.

'Good afternoon,' she said politely, then bent to kiss Connie's cheek as Luis shook hands with Tony and gave Claudio an affectionate clap on his shoulder.

After greeting Connie, Claudio burst out with his news in a torrent of Portuguese which Luis checked brusquely.

'You forget yourself, Claudio. Speak English, if you please, in Miss Kate's presence.'

Claudio threw Kate a penitent glance and calmed down a little as he informed his brother that Sofia had been waiting outside the school. '*É minha culpa não*—I mean it is not my fault!' he said passionately. 'I did not ask her to come—but Manoel Pires will kill me if he finds out.'

'*Calma, calma,*' said Luis, his face relaxing from the grim lines carved on it at the sight of Kate. 'At least I know you are now fluent in English, little brother!' He smiled. 'Perhaps so fluent that Miss Kate will allow you a little holiday. *Mamae* misses you, Claudio, and commands you to spend a few days with her in Parana.'

Claudio's face cleared like magic. He turned to Kate with a hopeful smile. 'You permit, Miss Kate?'

Kate smiled warmly. 'Of course. It's a brilliant idea, in the circumstances.'

Claudio, blissfully unaware of the tension between his brother and his English teacher, insisted on staying for coffee and cakes. And Connie, only too conscious of Kate's feelings, nevertheless could do no less than play the perfect hostess and press Luis to more coffee while he gave her news of his mother and the new nephew.

Since mention of Pascoa Vasconcelos acted like fire on Kate's skin she plunged into animated conversation with Tony and Claudio in an effort to drown out information she had no desire to hear. It was a relief when Luis rose to go, insisting that Claudio went home with him in the Mercedes.

'To keep you safe from lurking chefs armed with knives,' he said lightly, and Claudio, shuddering at the mere possibility, meekly made his farewells.

'I will send someone for the Fiat later, Connie,' said Luis as he kissed her cheek.

'That's all right, dear.' She smiled up at him anxiously. 'You look as though a good night's sleep wouldn't come amiss.'

'*É verdade, cara.*' He patted her cheek, then turned to Kate. '*Adeus*, Miss Kate. Thank you for allowing Claudio a holiday.'

Kate gave him a polite little smile. 'Not at all. The course finishes in two weeks anyway.'

A flash of emotion lit his eyes fleetingly. 'You leave so soon?'

'Yes.'

'You have enjoyed your time here?'

'Most of it very much,' said Kate quietly, then smiled at Claudio. 'If you call in at the school before you leave for Parana I'll give you some homework to do while you're away, Claudio.'

'You are cruel,' he sighed, then grinned. 'But I shall work hard. *Mamae* will be impressed.'

'Astonished, also,' said Luis drily, and after more goodbyes took his young brother off.

'Do you really think Claudio *is* in danger?' asked Connie anxiously.

'I fancy Luis does,' said Tony thoughtfully. 'I'd bet Claudio's trip to Parana was his idea; nothing to do with his mother.'

Kate made no comment, so upset over seeing Luis again that she went off to take a bath so she could get over it in private.

* * *

A couple of days later Tony went down with a virulent throat infection which landed him in hospital. Luis immediately put a car and driver at Connie's disposal to visit the invalid every day, though Kate was forbidden to go near Tony in case she caught the infection.

'No point you coming down with it as well, love,' said Connie firmly. 'I'm a nurse, remember, and I can make myself useful. Anyway, Tony's adamant you keep well away from him so you can cope with his share of the teaching as well as yours.'

Kate, knowing this was only sensible, agreed reluctantly, and merged both groups of students so that she could get through the prescribed work each day. And since Dinis drove Connie back from the hospital before coming to the school every day Kate took to preparing next day's work while she waited, supplied with coffee by Geraldo the caretaker, who never left the building until the *professora Inglêsa* was ready to do the same.

Of Luis Kate saw nothing after the first brief encounter on his return from Parana. It made no difference. The very fact that he was there in Vila Nova proved unsettling whether she saw him or not, which made the extra work welcome. She was only too pleased to feel fatigue every day if it meant she slept better, instead of tossing and turning until the small hours.

One day later Kate waited longer than usual for Dinis to arrive. By the time she'd prepared the next day's work and marked all the current day's essays, she began to feel uneasy. All the construction workers had left the site, and although Geraldo was still in the building she felt apprehensive once it was dark, and deeply worried that something must be seriously wrong with Tony. Her relief was enormous when the long-awaited headlights came into view at last through the darkness.

'Boa noite, Senhor Geraldo,' she called, gathering up her tote bag.

'Boa noite, senhora,' answered the man, who was on his rounds locking up. *'Até amanhã.'*

Kate ran across the uneven ground to find the Fiat waiting for her in place of the Mercedes. She stopped abruptly, her heart thumping as she saw Luis instead of Dinis at the wheel.

'Boa tarde, Kate,' he said quietly. 'Please get in the car.'

With undisguised reluctance Kate did as he said, hoping he couldn't see that her hands were shaking so much at the sight of him that she could hardly fasten her seatbelt. 'Good afternoon. Where's Dinis?'

'I sent him home,' Luis said briefly, keeping his eyes fixed firmly ahead after one brief look at her set face. 'I went to the hospital to see Tony, and found that Connie wishes to remain there for a while. They are short of staff, and she has volunteered to help with the daughter of one of her friends. The girl went into labour this afternoon. If you ring Elsa she will come back to stay the night with you if necessary.'

'I'll be fine on my own.'

'As you wish. I am merely relaying Connie's message, you understand.'

'Of course. Thank you. How was Tony?'

'He is better. The doctor says he should be much recovered by tomorrow. You may visit him then if you wish.'

'Thank goodness!' Kate let out a sigh of relief. 'I've felt horribly guilty about keeping away.'

'It was most necessary. Connie feared you would be infected, and Tony was anxious you remained well to take the classes.' Luis slowed as he caught sight of shadowy figures in the roadway, flagging him down. *'O que é isso?'*

Next moment he jammed on the brakes as one of the figures leapt directly in front of the bonnet, then both doors were wrenched open and Kate's scream stifled by an evil-smelling handkerchief thrust so hard into her open mouth that she gagged, her blood thundering in her ears as she felt an ice-cold blade against her windpipe seconds before a hood of some kind was dragged roughly over her head. She fought to free herself from hands which restrained her cruelly, while all the time a separate, silent struggle went on beside her in the close confines of the little car as Luis put up a desperate fight. His muffled, infuriated grunts indicated he was gagged as effectively as she, then he uttered a deep groan as a sickening thud put an abrupt end to the contest. Kate's scream of fear was muffled by the gag as her hands were bound tightly behind her back. Seconds later she was thrust on the floor in the back of the car with Luis's body on top of her, crushing the breath out of her, but quite definitely alive, to her passionate relief.

Kate gritted her teeth, determined to stay conscious as the car started up. One of the men slid into the back seat, his feet careless as they struck her shoulder, but Kate barely noticed the blow. All her energies were focused on trying to make out where they were headed, as the car, with its occupants still in chilling silence, proceeded along a road which she thought had to be the one beyond the school, in the opposite direction from Connie's house. A choked cry was wrenched from her as the car made a sudden, lurching turn on to what felt like a rough track, the bone-cracking jolting making it painfully clear that they were on a surface full of pot-holes. Kate felt sick and desperately frightened as the car bucked and jolted like a wild thing on its way to a destination she had no desire at all to reach, despite the discomfort of the journey. It was all too obvious they were being kidnapped, that a large ransom would be demanded in return for Luis Vasconcelos, *Patrão* of Minvasco. Black despair flooded Kate at the thought. Few kidnappers returned their hostages in mint condition, whether the ransom was paid or not.

Kate was in a sorry state by the time the car stopped. Rough hands hauled her out, prodding her to stand upright when her legs showed signs of giving way. The hood was raised slightly but only to allow contact of the knife-blade against her neck again as one of the kidnappers manhandled her over rough ground, hauling her along with a force which threatened to dislocate her shoulder as she stumbled along blindly. She could hear heavy panting from the man carrying Luis and they hadn't gone far before Kate was brought to a halt, a man's fingers like a manacle on her arm. She heard a key grate in a lock then she was thrust down a flight of stairs and propelled through a door with such force that she fell to the ground, choking on the gag as Luis was thrown on top of her once more.

Winded again, Kate lay helpless as a door slammed shut, chains rattled, a padlock clicked shut. She heard footsteps mounting stone steps, then another door

closed, and later, far in the distance, a car started up—
then there was nothing but thick, enveloping silence.

For a while she lay without moving a muscle, all
her energies concentrated on breathing normally in
circumstances which made it very difficult to breathe
at all. She must not, she told herself fiercely, give way
to panic. Her first priority must be to get out from
under Luis, who was squashing the life out of her.
Odd, thought Kate. When he'd been determined to
make love to her not so long ago he hadn't seemed
at all heavy as he lay on top of her. Now he felt like
a ton of bricks.

Inch by inch, pausing every minute or so to get her
breath, Kate wormed her way out from underneath
the tall, muscular body, desperately worried because
it felt so lifeless. Could that sickening blow have been
lethal after all? She felt a rush of panic, survived it,
then pulled herself together. No point in wondering
until she knew for certain. Then Kate brightened as
she realised that all her wriggling and slithering had
rucked the musty, smothering hood up as far as her
chin. If she persevered in rubbing against the suede
of Luis's jacket it was just possible she might get it
off entirely.

Kate had no idea how long the process took. By
the time she'd finally managed to shrug off the hood
she was sweating and exhausted and had a crick in
her neck, but as the sour-smelling material fell way
at last her triumph was like a surge of adrenalin in
the blood despite the disappointment of finding she
could see very little more than before. She was still
in total darkness but, thank heaven, she could breathe
more easily. Then her spirits rocketed as she heard a
faint groan. Luis was alive!

Kate almost gave way to tears at the discovery, but clamped down on the urge, reminding herself that crying would do her no good at all with a gag in her mouth. Instead she gave a silent prayer of thanks before taking stock of the situation. The air which she could breathe more freely now was cold and dank, it was true, but infinitely preferable to semi-asphyxia under that ghastly hood. And, Kate decided, since Luis was not dead as feared, things had taken a decided turn for the better, even if she did feel worn out after all that struggling and threshing about. Don't be so feeble, she ordered herself briskly, and thought hard about what she could do next.

The first thing, pretty obviously, was to find a way to free her hands. Kate was astonished by the effort it took to get to her feet with her hands tied behind her back. If ever she got out of this, she vowed bitterly, she'd take care to keep herself in better condition. By the time she was finally standing up her blood was roaring in her ears again, but her eyes had accustomed themselves a little to the darkness of their prison. By moving very cautiously, with her back to a cold stone wall, Kate found they were in some kind of basement. It was small and windowless, with only one door, which a sharp kick told her was a depressingly sturdy barrier to freedom. Then she discovered the presence of a bed of some sort by the simple process of bumping into it rather painfully, the same method revealing a rickety chair beside it, plus an upturned metal bucket.

At a groan from Luis she bent over him anxiously in the darkness, but as far as she could tell he was still unconscious. And was likely to remain that way unless she did something, Kate informed herself acidly. Sliding to a sitting position with a jarring thump in front of the bucket, she wriggled until it was jammed up against the wall behind her, blessing the fact that her captors had been in such a tearing hurry that they'd tied her wrists together so that her hands were parallel with each other, one palm to the back of the other hand. Now that her hands were numb with cold the rope was looser than it had been. Gritting her teeth, Kate pulled her hands apart as far as possible and began rubbing the rope back and forth across the sharp metal of the base of the bucket. She worked with a will, giving little smothered grunts of pain when bare skin met metal rim by mistake, but she persevered doggedly until at long last she felt one of the strands give way. Sweating and breathless, she had a rest, then heard faint, smothered sounds which indicated that Luis was showing signs of regaining consciousness. She kicked off one of her shoes, then rubbed her bare foot along his thigh in an attempt to soothe and reassure him, and received a grunt in response, which she hoped meant he was all right. Encouraged, she returned to her task.

Kate was thankful the cord used to tie her must have been old and frayed, since it finally gave way— after what seemed like hours it was true—but give way it did, and for a while she sat panting, her wrists swollen and on fire as she raised her hands up to wrench out the sickening gag.

'Luis!' she said hoarsely at once, going on her knees beside him as she drew off the muffling hood. 'Are you all right?'

He managed a choked sound in answer, and half sobbing with relief Kate tore the gag from his mouth and laid her cheek against his.

'Kate!' he said, his hoarse voice rough. 'Are you hurt? Did those sons of Satan molest you, *querida*?'

'No,' Kate said, as matter-of-factly as she could manage. She gave a shaky little laugh. 'Of course they stuffed a gag in my mouth, shoved a hood over my head at knife-point and tied my hands behind my back, but otherwise I'm fine. Turn over so I can untie your hands.'

Luis let out a stifled groan as he strove to obey. *'Graças a Deus,'* he panted. 'It has been hell lying here unable to ask if you were unharmed. What was the noise I heard? Like a tin can against a wall?'

'It's a quite wonderful metal bucket,' Kate told him blithely as her stiff fingers fumbled with the knots of a rope much stouter than the one used for her own wrists. At last she had it free and heard Luis gasp with pain as blood flowed back into his wrists.

'And what,' he said through clenched teeth, 'did you—do with—this so wonderful bucket?'

Kate explained at length, giving him time to recover as the feeling returned to his hands. 'Can you sit up now?' she asked.

'If you can, so can I,' he responded tightly.

'*I* didn't get knocked on the head.'

'I rejoice—to—hear it,' he said with difficulty as, breathing heavily, he heaved himself to a sitting position with his back against the unseen wall. 'For me—it is the second such—blow recently.'

Kate blushed unseen in the darkness. 'How do you feel?'

'Cold!' he said, teeth chattering.

Now she had time to think about it Kate found she was cold, too. 'Next time I get kidnapped I'll bring a flask of coffee and an overcoat...' Her voice thickened, and to her dismay she found she wanted to cry again.

'Will you misunderstand if I suggest we stay close together?' said Luis gruffly. 'For warmth, you understand.'

'Good idea! There's a sort of bed. If we sit on that, we'd be away from this horribly cold wall.'

'Pois é,' he said in a stifled voice. *'Disculpe-me,* Kate, but I have no feeling in my fingers yet. If you could look in my pocket you will find a lighter. It will help if we can see where we are going.'

'Brilliant!' she said in delight, and moved close to reach into his pocket for the lighter. By its small flame they surveyed each other in silence. 'You look awful, Luis,' she said anxiously. 'There's blood on your forehead.'

He shrugged, smiling at her. 'If I am bleeding I am alive, *não é*?'

With the aid of the tiny flame Kate helped Luis to his feet and led him towards the bed, which was a rough frame with wooden slats and a mattress rolled at one end.

'We're in luck,' she said brightly, as she shook out the mattress, which was stained and malodorous, but better than the wooden slats or stone floor.

Neither of them said anything for a while once they'd slumped together in a huddle on the bed, in darkness again to conserve their only means of light. Kate, painfully aware of her sore, swollen wrists, leaned against Luis limply, thankful for simple human contact now that she had time to consider the bleakness of their prospects.

'Are our kidnappers after money, do you think?' she asked at last.

Luis stirred sufficiently to slide his arm cautiously around her waist. '*Sem duvida, carinha*. Why else would they imprison me? Because,' he added bitterly, 'it was an unhappy accident that you were with me. I do not believe you were part of their plan.'

'They won't get much money in exchange for me, that's for sure,' Kate agreed lightly.

'*Deus!*' said Luis with sudden violence, his arm tightening about her. 'I would give my soul to have you safely at home instead of here with me like this.' He breathed in sharply. 'But regrets will not get us out of here. I feel stronger now. Let me investigate our prison.'

With the help of the lighter Luis confirmed that the door was a heavy affair which, when rattled, proved to have a chain and padlock on the other side. Otherwise he learned little more than Kate had in the dark.

'We are in a cellar,' said Luis breathlessly, quite plainly glad to sit down again. 'I feel I should know this place. Were you conscious on the journey, Kate? Did we travel far?'

'I don't think so. We went along the road beyond the school for a bit, I think, then the car turned off on a very rough track full of pot-holes.' Kate gave a little chuckle. 'You were on top of me and nearly knocked the breath out of me in places.'

'*Perdoneme*, Kate!' He laughed a little. 'If we had to travel in such a fashion, I must regret I was unconscious!'

Kate ignored him. 'Then we stopped a short distance from this place. It was very rough ground. They were puffing and panting as they carried you, and very cross every time I stumbled. Then they pushed us down the stairs here, locked us in and you know the rest.' She felt him raise his free hand, then he cursed softly.

'My watch is broken, Kate. Are you wearing one?'

Kate's was a large, workmanlike affair, with blessedly luminous hands which showed it was nearly ten o'clock. 'Good heavens,' she said, troubled. 'I didn't realise it was so late. I hope Connie's not at home yet—she'll be frantic!'

'Our captors may have already contacted Minvasco to ask for a ransom,' Luis said quietly.

Kate gulped. 'In which case she'll be even more frantic!' Suddenly she stiffened. 'Luis! I can hear a car.'

'Quickly, *querida*,' he said urgently. 'Tie my hands roughly, then put the hoods over our heads and keep your hands behind your back. Let them think we are still helpless.'

Kate worked like lightning. By the time the expected footsteps sounded on the stone steps they were both lying on the floor again. She felt Luis tense against her as the door opened, then there was a clank of metal as something was dumped on the floor. Rough hands removed her hood in the darkness. She heard sounds which suggested a similar office was being performed for Luis, then she saw figures moving against the glow of a torch outside the door. Suddenly one of the men bent over her. Kate heard a hiss of surprise, then blinked owlishly as a torch shone in her eyes.

'*Santa Maria!*' howled one of the men. '*O que é isso?*' The torch swung in Luis's direction, and one look at the dark, menacing face of Luis Vasconcelos sent the men into a stampede of panic as they rushed from the room, their flood of mutual recrimination totally unintelligible to Kate as they padlocked the door and tore up the stairs. As Kate pulled the gag from her mouth she heard a car in the distance, screaming off into the night like a banshee as their captors gunned the engine in their frantic desire to be away.

'What on earth was all that about?' she demanded as she removed Luis's gag.

'We are the wrong hostages,' he said grimly. 'They thought they had Claudio and Sofia.'

Kate gasped. 'Are you sure?'

'You may not have understood them, *carinha*, but I did. I could not see their faces—they wore masks. But I think one of them was Manoel Pires. Sofia must have run away, and Manoel thinks she is with Claudio.' He punched a fist into the palm of his hand. '*É claro*, Kate. I was driving the Fiat tonight, it was dark, they mistook me for Claudio and you for Sofia.'

'Must have been a nasty shock for them when they realised who you were!'

Luis uttered a grim laugh in the darkness. '*É verdade!* A shock indeed to discover they had kidnapped the man who was to provide the ransom money.'

'So what do we do now?'

'We wait until daylight, Kate, which is when they mean to return. By then,' he added softly, 'I shall be in better condition to deal with them.'

Cold trickles ran down Kate's spine at the prospect. 'Give me your lighter, please, Luis. I think they've left us some food.'

The little flame revealed an enamel plate of bread and elderly cheese, also a small bottle of some clear liquid which Luis, after one sniff, told her was *cachaça*.

'It is raw cane spirit. Not everyone's taste, but it will keep us warm.'

He was right. One sip was like downing a live coal. Kate gasped for breath, spluttering and laughing.

'Good grief—now I know what they mean by fire-water!' She curled up on the bed beside Luis, her back to the wall. 'I feel better already. Amazing, isn't it, what a difference a spot of food and drink can do?'

Luis stretched, wincing a little as his bruises throbbed, then he slid his arm round her. 'It seems our captors do not mean to starve us, yes. So now we huddle together to conserve the warmth, and resign ourselves to wait for dawn.'

Kate wriggled closer, shivering. 'Do you think they mean to kill us, Luis?'

'No. I think they will come to bargain. Our lives in return for their freedom, also money. Dead I am useless. Alive I am the source of a new life for them in some other country.' In the darkness he put a hand under her chin and raised her face to his. 'Do not be afraid, *querida*. I shall not let them harm you.' He laughed suddenly. 'But of *course* you are not afraid! You, who free yourself from ropes and gags, are the one who rescues me, *não é*? My beautiful little Amazon!'

Kate felt his breath warm against her cheek and turned her face up to him blindly in the darkness. Luis tensed for a second, then caught her close, his mouth finding hers with a hunger which brought their fragile barrier crashing down to leave nothing between them but the glad realisation that they were together and, for the moment at least, they were alive.

CHAPTER NINE

THE kiss began as a means of comfort and consolation. That it failed to remain so came as no great surprise to either of them. Both Kate and Luis found themselves at the mercy of emotions heightened to fever pitch by the events of the evening, by the certainty at one point that they might not survive to kiss anyone again, let alone each other. Their quarrel was forgotten, their differences melting like magic in the heat of holding each other close, mouth against mouth, tongue finding tongue as heartbeats accelerated and breathing quickened. Life was reduced at one stroke to basic need for each other, to thanksgiving for the wonderful gift of being together, battered and bruised and filthy, but marvellously, electrifyingly alive.

'*Deus, querida,*' muttered Luis, tearing his mouth from hers after a while. 'I do not want——'

'Don't you?' she whispered against his lips. 'I do. So very much.'

The man who had made no complaint during his ordeal groaned like a soul in torment. 'You know—*Deus*, you can *feel*—that I desire you so much I am burning up with it, *amada*. But it would not be right——'

'Right!' she said violently. 'We could have died tonight. Perhaps we *will* die in the morning——'

She got no further. His mouth stifled any further arguments as Luis Vasconcelos, oblivious of a head which throbbed, of wrists chafed and sore from the rope, forgot everything in the world other than the warm, living presence of the girl in his arms.

And Catherine Ashley, filthy and battered like her lover, surrendered to him with a joyous abandon which quenched any last, lingering doubts he might have had about taking the gift she offered. With no trace of self-consciousness Kate pulled her sweater over her head briskly before rolling it into a pillow for their inelegant bed, while Luis stripped off his jacket and shirt at top speed to spread them on the mattress before lying full length with Kate on the narrow cot, both of them laughing and breathless as they clung close to avoid falling on the floor.

'There must be some other way——' gasped Kate.

'There is,' said Luis simply, and slid her gently beneath him, and abruptly they were silent.

Slowly, languorously, Kate slid her arms round his neck as his mouth met hers, while Luis, with a dexterity she only dimly noticed at the time, removed what remained of their clothes without taking his lips from hers except to slide them over her face in a series of little fire-raising kisses.

'You crushed the life out me before. Why aren't you so heavy now?' she muttered feverishly, as her head threshed to and fro on the makeshift pillow as his marauding mouth found her breasts.

He laughed softly and moved his mouth lower. 'It is magic, *encantadora*. Magic we make together, you and I.'

Kate soon found Luis was right. The spell they wove together proved powerful enough to transform their cold, dark prison into a place of enchantment, where all was fire and delight as Luis caressed and cajoled every nerve and fibre of her responsive body into joyous life. At last, when she could endure the hot, sweet anguish no longer, he slid one hand into her hair, his mouth against her throat as their bodies slotted together with such ravishing exactitude that Kate had no attention to spare for the small, searing pain of the first moment of union. All life became centred on the rapture which followed as her expert lover swept her along with him in a surging, inexorable drive for fulfilment.

Luis held her close as the shock waves subsided, muttering things in her ear which Kate was sure would be gratifying if she could only understand them.

'I've learnt *some* Portuguese,' she informed him breathlessly, 'but my vocabulary doesn't cover a situation like this.'

He buried his face in her hair. 'I was telling you how perfect an experience this was for me, how I wished our first loving could have been in a a place more worthy of it——'

'But if we hadn't been locked up in this particular place our—our loving would never have happened,' she pointed out, and winced.

He raised his head in alarm. *'Que foi, meu amor?'*

'Remember that magic you talked about?' she said ruefully. 'It's worn off a bit. You feel like a ton of bricks again.'

'Perdoneme, Kate!' He rolled over cautiously, taking her with him so that she lay against his chest. 'We must dress. You will be cold.'

'OK. In a minute,' she said sleepily. 'I'm so *tired*, Luis.'

He laughed unsteadily. 'It is not surprising, *querida*. Any other woman I know would be in a state of collapse after the treatment you have suffered from those *canalhos*.' His arms tightened round her convulsively. 'Then to make love together as we just did was miraculous but also exhausting, *não é*?'

'*Very* exhausting.' She yawned, and wriggled closer, but Luis insisted she dress, then hurried into his own clothes, cursing under his breath as various bruises made themselves felt. He pulled his suede jacket over them, then held Kate as close to him as he could on the narrow pallet, and, in spite of aches and pains and the discomfort of their makeshift bed, they were soon deeply asleep in each other's arms.

Kate woke in the dark, stiff and disorientated. She reached out empty arms in alarm. 'Luis! Where are you?'

'Here, *carinha*.' At once Luis let himself down beside her, holding her close. 'You are shivering. You will be ill.'

'Yes, I am and no, I won't,' she said, burrowing against him. 'I thought for a moment I was alone.'

He laughed softly, holding her closer. 'Where would I have gone?'

'I don't know. I just felt cold without your arms around me.'

'I have been awake for some time. I took the lighter to examine our prison again, Kate. It is larger than I thought. What time is it?'

Kate peered at her watch. 'Nearly four.'

'Soon—much too soon—it will be dawn.'

'That's when they'll be back,' she said apprehensively.

'Yes, Kate. So I want you to think very hard. When the car turned off into the rougher road, which way did it turn? To the left or to the right?'

'To the right. My head bumped against the right-hand door of the car as it turned.'

'*Bem*—I think I know where we are. Not very far away is an old, disused gold mine—Mina de Lobo. Our prison, I think, used to be a store belonging to the mine.'

'What kind of store—a shop?'

He shook his head, rubbing his cheek against hers. 'It is a—a powder house. Where the explosives were stored. Therefore it is made of stone instead of the adobe which would have been much easier to escape from, you understand.' He breathed in deeply, then kissed her hard before continuing. 'The door is several centimetres thick, there is no window and the walls are made of stone. I can do nothing—nothing!' he groaned in angry frustration. 'My only plan is to wait until the men return, when I shall try to overpower them in some way.'

'You'll do no such thing!' she contradicted sharply, whereupon Luis embarked on a heated explanation of why he had no alternative but to attack the kidnappers the moment they came through the door while Kate ran like the wind to safety.

'It is not far to Vila Nova,' he said urgently. 'If you run to your left the moment you leave here you will reach a track which will take you back to the main road. Do not fear. If there are only two of them I can occupy them easily until you escape.'

Kate told him what she thought of his plan in no uncertain terms. They argued fiercely for several minutes, until Luis put an end to the argument by kissing her again.

'Let us not waste our time together in fighting, *querida*,' he muttered against her mouth, and Kate, much struck by the sense of this, agreed so whole-heartedly that it was only moments before they were undressing each other in feverish haste, everything forgotten expect their need of each other as they discovered a wonder even greater than before.

'So should end all arguments,' said Luis hoarsely when he could speak.

'Amen,' agreed Kate. Her lips curved in a smile against his throat. 'With each other, anyway.'

'Isso mesmo!' he said fervently. 'Do not attempt it with any other man.'

'OK, I won't.' Kate moved away a little, her breath catching as she looked at her watch. 'Luis—it's almost time.'

They scrambled hurriedly into their clothes, then sat close in each other's arms to await whatever fate had in store as dawn broke.

'Deus, why do I not have a knife or a gun—or even a rock?' cursed Luis bitterly, at one point. 'What a hero!'

Kate touched a hand to his stubbled jaw. 'If I have to be in a place like this, in circumstances like these, Luis Vasconcelos, you're the only man in the world I want with me.'

'Meu amor!' he breathed against her cheek, then gave her a long kiss subtly different from those of a few minutes earlier. Kate felt a thrill of fear as she realised that this might be the last kiss they would ever exchange. Suddenly he tensed against her. 'I hear a car!' He put her away from him gently as footsteps descended the stairs outside the door. There was a long, tense silence, while Kate's heart beat so loudly she was sure the man outside must hear it.

At last a voice spoke outside the door. 'Senhor Vasconcelos?'

'Quem fala?' asked Luis harshly.

'Manoel Pires.'

Kate could see Luis plainly by this time, as light filtered through a grating high up in the door. He looked unfamiliar, like a filthy, dishevelled stranger as he stared at the door with eyes which burned in his grim face. The tension in his posture communicated itself to Kate as she experienced real, spine-chilling terror for the first time in the whole escapade.

Had Manoel Pires really come to kill them? She clenched her teeth to stop them chattering. Looking at it logically he had little real choice. He could hardly expect to get away scot-free after kidnapping the head of Companhia Minvasco.

'Coragem, meu amor,' said Luis softly, and Kate straightened her shoulders, taking in a deep, steadying breath as he moved very quietly towards the door.

The following few minutes were the longest and most frustrating of Kate's life. Unable to understand more than a word or two of the oddly unimpassioned exchange conducted through the heavy door, she was helpless to do anything but wait for an eventual translation. She watched Luis fearfully as, face intent, he listened to the other man, thought for a while, then answered in calm, uninflected tones which gave no indication as to what was happening.

At last Luis turned to Kate, and told her that Manoel Pires had not been one of the pair who'd abducted them the night before. The culprits, old friends of the chef, had decided to teach the faithless Sofia a lesson she would never forget. After seeing her hanging about at the school, waiting to see Claudio, they hit on the plan of staging a mock-kidnapping.

'They intended merely to take the girl and leave her here overnight to frighten her out of her wits,' said Luis. 'Claudio was to be abandoned, blindfolded and tied up in the car like a trussed cockerel outside the school for the construction workers to find this morning. But one of the men, whom Manoel refuses to name, had an *inspiração*. How much better to kidnap Claudio for real, to demand money from me to get him back!' He gave a bark of mirthless laughter. 'When they found they'd kidnapped you and me by mistake, Kate, they panicked, drove to Manoel in Belo Horizonte and borrowed money to escape to anonymity somewhere in the *mata*—some Godforsaken part of this great country where no questions are asked.'

'So what now?' asked Kate, her eyes trusting as they looked up into his.

'He says he has a gun,' said Luis, looking towards the door. 'But swears he will not use it if I promise not to call the police.'

'Do you trust him?'

Luis turned oddly absent eyes on her. 'I have no choice but to trust him. He is a good man. I know his family well. If I had not had regard for Manoel I would not have been so forbearing when he stabbed Claudio. Yet to let him go free a second time!' He shrugged, his face grim. 'It is lenient to the point of *loucura*—lunacy.'

'What happens if you don't give him the promise?' said Kate, swallowing.

'For myself I would take my chance on disarming him,' said Luis with vehemence. 'It is an intolerable

insult to my pride to suffer assault and imprisonment!' His eyes glittered in the faint light. 'But I have
you, Kate.' He thrust a hand through his hair. '*Deus*,
what it is to feel so helpless!'

Kate regarded him anxiously, disturbed by the rage
and frustration behind the mask of calm he was
struggling to maintain. 'If you promise, what then?'

'He says he will take Sofia to Argentina, find work
there.' Luis pulled her into his arms with sudden fer-
ocity. 'I have no choice, Kate. I am forced to
promise—even as my pride revolts at so tame a
solution.'

To blazes with pride, thought Kate. The mere idea
of Luis wrestling with an armed man brought her out
in a cold sweat. 'Promise, and get it over with,' she
said tersely. 'Be sensible, for heaven's sake!'

Luis exchanged a few short, harsh sentences with
the man on the other side of the door. He stood back,
motioning Kate away as the padlock and chain were
removed, then, just as the door began to open, Luis
wrenched it inwards, taking Manoel Pires off guard
and punched him viciously on the jaw, sending the
man sprawling on the stone floor at Kate's feet.

'Get the gun!' rapped out Luis, standing over the
fallen man.

Kate, more shocked by Luis's action than anything
she'd endured so far, goggled at him in appalled
silence.

'Find the *gun*!' he shouted impatiently, then bent
to glare into the face of the groaning man as he re-
gained consciousness. '*O pistola, Manoel. Agora!*'

Manoel Pires gave a hopeless little shrug as he lay
staring up in trepidation at the man towering over him.

'Nao tenho pistola, Senhor Vasconcelos,' he said miserably. *'Foi mentira.'*

Luis Vasconcelos glared incensed at the hapless young man as he told Kate the gun had been non-existent after all.

'Rather like your promise,' she said coldly.

Luis stared at her in astonishment. 'I have broken no promise.'

'That's not what it looks like from here!'

Manoel looked from one to another in dazed incomprehension, his face blanching as the full light of day illuminated the room where the *Patrão* of Minvasco had been incarcerated all night.

Luis drew himself up to his full height, looking down his nose at Kate with an expression reminiscent of the oil-paintings at Casa dos Sonhos. 'I *promised* I would not call the police. I gave my word—the word of a Vasconcelos. But I gave no promise not to knock his stupid teeth down his throat. You expect me to stand meekly by like an idiot and do nothing at all when I have been offered such insult? Not only has injury been caused to my brother and to myself, but through Manoel and his wretched Sofia fear and distress was experienced by my woman——'

'By *who*?' said Kate, eyes kindling.

'My woman,' repeated Luis softly, his eyes locked with hers until a deprecating cough reminded him Manoel was still lying at his feet. *'Levanta!'* he snapped, and hauled the man to his feet, letting loose a torrent of invective in his own tongue, which, instead of sending the man plummeting to the depths of depression, seemed to open the gates of paradise. Manoel Pires, who was little more than a boy, now Kate could see him properly, showered profuse,

hysterical thanks on Luis Vasconcelos, handed over
the Fiat keys then fled up the stone stairs to freedom.

Luis watched him go with a scowl on his dust-
streaked face, then held out a hand to Kate. *'Vamos,'*
he said wearily. 'Let us go home.'

Kate was trembling with fatigue and reaction as she
followed Luis out of the stone powder house into the
radiance of early morning. She looked back at the
small building, which stood, semi-derelict and over-
grown with vegetation, on a track which led into what
looked like the back of beyond. She was given no time
to gaze at the scene of the most momentous night of
her life. Luis strode ahead without a backward glance,
supremely confident, it seemed, that she was following
behind.

By the time they reached the Fiat both of them were
too weary to speak, even if either had been inclined
to do so. Kate made rather a business of fastening her
seatbelt as Luis started the car, and afterwards stared
dumbly at the red dusty surface of the track which
led for a couple of miles before they rejoined the main
road into Vila Nova. What, thought Kate drearily,
would they have found to talk about anyway, in the
circumstances? Last night they had both feared it
might be their last on earth. Otherwise, Kate assured
herself, she would never have allowed Luis to make
love to her.

Come off it, she sneered at herself silently. There'd
been no *allowing* about it. She'd been just as eager
as Luis. She bit her lip. One couldn't even look on it
in the light of an accident. Once would have been an
accident. Twice was not. Kate tensed as they came in
sight of Casa Londres. Now for it, she thought

miserably. Connie was bound to be out of her mind with worry after a sleepless night. Probably the police were out combing the countryside at this very moment. Kate shuddered. What a mess!

They climbed from the car to a tumultuous welcome from Bruno, who frolicked riotously from the grim, dishevelled man to the weary girl, disappointed when they refused to play with him.

'Down, Bruno,' said Kate dispiritedly. She looked up at the quiet house in surprise. There was no sign of a demented Connie after all, nor of anyone else. She turned to Luis. 'Are you coming in?'

'*Pois é,*' he said distantly, as he followed her up the steps. 'Do you think I would abandon you to make explanations alone?'

Kate found the house locked, with no sign of Connie. She had to rummage in her handbag for keys she'd never had to use before as she unlocked the door leading from the veranda into the hall. She cast an uncertain look in Luis's direction.

'I'll just see if she's still in bed.'

He frowned, rubbing his chin. 'I am surprised. I thought she would be pacing up and down in anguish because you were missing.'

Kate gave a rueful grin. 'So did I, frankly. I'm glad she's not upset, of course, but I must say it's a bit of a let-down.' She knocked on Connie's bedroom door, then peered round it cautiously, her eyes widening as she saw the bed hadn't been slept in. She went back to Luis.

'Either she's up early or she wasn't home last night.'

They stared at each other.

'Shall I go, then?' asked Luis. 'Are you afraid to remain alone?'

'Afraid?' she snapped. 'After all that happened last night you think I'm afraid of mere solitude?'

'I would prefer to wait until the maid comes.'

'No!' Kate bit her lip as her refusal rapped out more vehemently than intended. 'I'd rather you didn't.'

The handsome, grimy face darkened. 'Then I shall leave at once,' he said stiffly.

'Won't you let me clean up that cut on your head a little before...?' Kate tensed as a car drew up in the road outside. She hurried out on the veranda at the sound of Connie's Anglicised Portuguese bidding someone farewell, her throat thickening as she saw the slim, familiar figure come hurrying up the drive. Connie halted in surprise as she saw the small Fiat parked near the steps. She looked up, her face wreathed in smiles as she saw Kate and Luis.

'You're about early this morning, Luis!' she said as she came running up the steps. 'What a night! It was twins in the end, and would the second one hurry? I thought he'd *never* get born, and there was the poor little mum, exhausted, but still with enough breath to scream her head off...'

Connie trailed into silence as her eyes took in the appearance of the other two, her smile fading.

'Oh, my goodness—whatever's happened? Did someone break in, darling? Are you all right, Kate? And you, Luis, what have you done to your head and why are you both so filthy——?'

'Come inside, Connie,' said Luis, urging both women into the *sala*.

Kate opened her mouth to begin some kind of explanation, but burst into tears instead and fell into Connie's arms, after which there was no nonsense about explanations or anything else. Having begun to cry Kate found it impossible to stop until she was dosed with brandy and hot tea and a lot of loving scolding from Connie as Luis gave a brief, unimpassioned account of their abduction and imprisonment, followed by their unexpected escape. Connie went red then white, as she listened, clutching Kate in her arms as though she expected the abductors to reappear any moment to wrest the girl away from her.

'May I telephone Casa dos Sonhos?' Luis asked at last.

'Of course, dear!' She looked up at him shrewdly. 'Do you think one of those men rang there last night?'

He shrugged. *'É possível. Com licença.'* He went from the room to use the telephone in the hall, while Connie turned Kate's tear-blotched face up to hers.

'Those men, love. The ones who abducted you. Did they interfere with you?'

'Interfere?' Kate managed a wavering grin. 'Oh— no. No—they didn't. They thought I was Sofia, remember.'

'What difference does that make?'

'Her swain's far too handy with a knife, Connie!'

Kate dissolved into laughter which threatened to get hysterical until Connie gave her a brisk tap on her cheek and ordered her to stop all that just as Luis came back into the room.

'No one contacted my home or the office,' he said, shrugging. 'Manoel must have intervened before they could make any demands for money.' He gave a snort of disgust. *'Que bagunça!'*

'If you mean farce, I agree,' said Kate quietly, looking away. 'A total comedy of errors one way and another.'

'You are better, Kate?' he asked.

'I'm fine.' She looked at him fleetingly. 'Didn't anyone at your home wonder where you were last night?'

Dull colour rose along his cheekbones. 'No.' He shrugged. 'It is not unknown for me to spend the night away from Casa dos Sonhos.'

Kate flushed scarlet, thankful when Connie took Luis off to the bathroom to wash and dress the wound on his temple. Glad to be alone for a moment, Kate went to the window to watch the sun rising over the hills behind Vila Nova. It was a beautiful day, she thought despondently. A day she had thought, at one point, that she might never see. Odd really that she felt so depressed now the danger was over, particularly when she and Luis had never even been missed.

'I must go now, Kate,' said Luis behind her and she turned to see him watching her intently, looking a lot better for a wash, but tired and drawn beneath the dressing taped to his forehead. Connie, by the clatter of dishes in the kitchen, was keeping tactfully out of the way.

'Goodbye,' said Kate.

He moved closer, his eyes urgent. 'We must talk later.'

She frowned slightly. 'Why?'

'*Why?*' He scowled blackly. 'There is much to discuss.'

'I don't see what, exactly.' Kate pushed her hair back wearily. 'Good thing it's Saturday,' she said, yawning suddenly. 'I don't think I could cope with my class today.'

'You need give no more lessons,' Luis said sharply.

Kate stared at him blankly. 'I haven't finished the course yet.'

'I am sure your students already speak sufficient English for my purpose. I wish you to spend the remaining time as a holiday. I will put a car at your disposal and you and Connie, Tony also when he recovers, may visit whatever local places of interest you wish.'

'Thank you for the offer, but I can't do that,' she said flatly. 'I came here with a job to do and I intend to finish it.'

Luis breathed in deeply, his jaw clenched. 'The situation is different now, Kate,' he said with dangerous calm.

She frowned. 'I don't see why.'

'You can say such a thing after—after last night!'

'But no one seems to know about it. Manoel won't talk, and the other two are probably somewhere up the Amazon by now. Why shouldn't I carry on as normal?'

Luis seized her hands, then dropped them at the sound of Connie's footsteps in the hall. 'I will come to see you tonight, after dinner,' he said urgently. 'Perhaps Connie will allow me some time alone with you.'

'There's nothing to discuss——' began Kate, then fell silent as Connie joined them, very much the ward sister as she took them in hand.

'Come on, you two. Luis, I think it's time Kate had a bath and a sleep. You could do with the same, by the look of you.'

Luis managed a smile with palpable effort, and took his leave with as good grace as he could muster after winning Connie's permission to call back that evening.

'Right,' said Connie after he'd gone. She fixed Kate with shrewd blue eyes. 'Now then, my girl. Let's hear what really happened!'

CHAPTER TEN

KATE went along on the hospital visit to Tony later that afternoon, after deciding with Connie on a suitably edited version of her kidnap.

'You look a bit rough, Kate,' said Tony in alarm, after Connie went off to check on her twins. 'Not coming down with the dreaded lurgy, I hope?'

Kate explained her haggard appearance by giving Tony a light-hearted account of her adventure, which caused him no end of excitement as he plied her with questions, cursing himself for missing all the fun.

'Fun!' said Kate bitterly. 'If you weren't still poorly I'd show you my bruises!'

Tony sobered. He shot a troubled look at her. 'Are you OK? I mean, there wasn't—they didn't...?'

'No, they didn't!' snapped Kate. 'Let's change the subject. When are they letting you out?'

Because Tony was staying at the hotel the doctor wouldn't release him until a day or so later.

'After they've stopped jabbing me in the rear with antibiotics,' said Tony glumly, then brightened. 'Mind you, there's a rather gorgeous nurse on night duty.'

Kate grinned. 'Make sure she doesn't have a knife-happy lover lurking somewhere, or your throat might be the least of your problems!'

Dinner that evening was not a success. The prawns in their hot, spicy sauce were delicious, so was the accompanying salad and the coconut ice-cream which followed, but Kate couldn't eat any of it, however hard she tried.

'Kate,' said Connie gently. 'You can't live on tea. You've had nothing else all day.'

'I know. Silly, isn't it?' Kate leaned her chin in her hands in despair. 'I just can't swallow.'

'You've been like a cat on hot bricks ever since we came home.'

'I just wish Luis hadn't insisted on coming tonight, that's all.'

'It's only natural, love, in the circumstances.' Connie refilled Kate's teacup. 'He'll want to make sure you're all right after the fright you had.'

Kate turned to Connie impulsively. 'Couldn't you say I'm *not* all right? That I've taken to my bed with a virus, or something?'

Connie refused to be a party to any such deceit, and when eight o'clock came she was firmly installed in her own room with one of Kate's novels and her record player.

'Which I shall turn up loud so I can't hear a thing,' she said, as she waved Kate away at the sound of the car.

Kate, dressed formally for once in silk shirt and tailored dark skirt, watched from the semi-darkness of the veranda as the Mercedes nosed through the gate and cruised to a stop at the foot of the steps. She smiled wryly as Luis took time to make a fuss of the dog before mounting the steps to the veranda. As he caught sight of Kate watching him from the shadows he stopped abruptly. 'I did not see you there. *Boa tarde*, Kate. How do you feel this evening?'

'I'm fine. I thought we might stay out here for a while. It's such a beautiful night it seems a shame to go indoors.'

'Will you not be cold?' he asked as he held a wicker chair for her.

'If I do there's one of Connie's hand-knitted shawls at the ready. Guaranteed to keep out worse cold than you have here in Minas Gerais.' Kate waved a hand at the tray on the table in front of them. 'Can I pour you some Scotch?'

'*Obrigad*'. A small amount only.' Luis sat down in the chair nearest Kate, his eyes on her face. He took the glass she offered him and raised it in toast. 'To the miracle of being alive, Kate.'

'Amen to that!'

There was a small silence while they both eyed each other like combatants sizing up the opposition. Luis looked a different man from the haggard, dirty stranger of the morning. He wore a formal light grey suit, his shirt gleaming pristine under the veranda lantern, which picked up gleams of light in the walnut gloss of his hair and a look of such determination on his face that Kate felt deep foreboding.

'Where is Connie?' asked Luis.

'She insisted on shutting herself up in her room with a book.' Kate stared out at the stars. 'I didn't ask her to.'

'By the sound of your voice,' he said drily, 'it is plain you begged her to stay.'

Since this was no more than the truth Kate had no answer for him. The silence between them became so prolonged that she could hear rustlings in the garden above the familiar evening chorus of the crickets.

'You are very quiet, Kate,' said Luis at last. 'You wish me to go?'

'No—no, of course not!'

'That is good, because I do not intend to go until I have said what I have come to say.'

Kate shifted in her seat uneasily. 'You don't have to say anything at all, Luis. It wasn't your fault that we got attacked.'

'*É verdade*. But it was entirely my fault that I took advantage of the situation to seduce you.' He flung the words down between them like a gauntlet.

Kate flinched, then sat very straight in her chair. 'Since you find it necessary to bring the subject up I feel it only right to point out that seduction is not the word for what happened between us. It suggests some unwillingness on my part, and—and there wasn't any. None at all.'

'I had hoped so very much to hear you say that, *carinha*.' His voice took on a new note, warm now with assurance. 'I should not, I know well, have tried to make love to you, but the events of the night proved too much for my self-control.'

'Hardly surprising, really,' she said lightly. 'You'd been mugged and tied up and gagged. No one could blame you for what happened in the circumstances.'

'I blame myself,' he said bitterly.

'But I don't, Luis. We both thought we might die in the morning. I'm sure no one would blame us for taking what comfort we could from the situation.'

'*Comfort!*' He sprang to his feet and went to lean at the veranda rail. 'Is that all it was for you, Kate?'

'You know perfectly well it was a great deal more than that.'

Luis turned to stare down at her. 'I had not expected to be your first lover, Kate.'

Hot colour surged over her in a tide as she stared down at her tightly clasped hands. 'Why not?'

'You are twenty-five and very beautiful. I dared not hope—I mean, I did not expect——'

'If you had known would it have stopped you last night?' she cut in.

'No. You know well it would not. At the time I could think of nothing in the world but how much I desired you, and when I found you desired me in return nothing on earth or in heaven could have stopped me from taking you, *querida*.'

With a swift, graceful movement he leaned down to pull her to her feet so that she stood close against his chest, with only their clasped hands keeping them apart. She could feel the tension vibrating in his body, the warmth of him, the scent of his skin which, Kate realised with a jolt, she would recognise blindfolded.

'And because I took so unexpected and precious a gift from you, *meu amor*, I wish to pay for it in the time-honoured way,' he said caressingly.

Kate stiffened. '*Pay* for it? What the devil do you mean?'

'Do not swear at me, little spitfire.' He laughed softly. 'I did not mean money—not directly, *sem duvida*.'

Kate tried to pull away, but he held her fast. 'I don't need payment of any kind,' she said hotly. 'What happened happened. I'm not blaming *you* for it.'

'*Escuta*, Kate. Listen to me!' He shook her slightly, then dropped her hands and pulled her so close she could feel the thud of his heart against her. 'I am offering you marriage, *amada*.'

Kate stiffened. 'Marriage?' she said incredulously. 'Why?'

'*Deus me livre*, Kate!' He raised her face to his and looked deep into her eyes. 'After last night you still ask why?'

Kate detached herself firmly and stepped away. 'Come into the *sala*, Luis. I think we need some light.'

Inside Connie's sitting-room they stood facing each other, one either side of the fireplace, where twin wall-lamps shed a clear light on both tense faces as Kate returned to the attack.

'Now. Tell me exactly *why* you're asking me to marry you.'

His eyes narrowed. 'I do not know how such things are conducted in *Inglaterra*, Kate. Possibly our customs here seem strange to you. After last night what alternative can there be but marriage between you and me?'

'Why? No one knows about it *except* you and me—and Connie.' Her mouth curved in a disdainful smile. 'One can hardly count Manoel. He's not likely to land himself in any trouble by spilling the beans.' She shrugged impatiently at his blank look. 'By telling anyone, I mean.'

'So. Since no one knows all is well.' Luis took his cigar-case from his pocket. 'You permit?'

There was silence while Luis regarded her at length through a thin veil of smoke. 'And Tony. You have told him of—of our adventure?'

'Yes. It brightened up visiting time at the hospital no end,' said Kate flippantly.

'Was *he* not concerned that we had spent the night together alone?'

She laughed scornfully. 'Come off it, Luis! This is the twentieth century. Besides...' She paused, flushing a little. 'It didn't even occur to him that you would—well...'

'Harm you?'

'You didn't harm me!' She faced him squarely. 'Luis, tell me the truth, please.'

'*Pois é*, Kate. What do you want to know?'

'This proposal of marriage. Would you have made it if last night had never happened?'

The dark, handsome face drained of expression as Luis stared into the luminous eyes locked with his.

'There is no point in asking such a question,' he said at last, as though the words were being hacked out of him. 'But it can be no secret, Kate, that I have desired you from the first. You are a woman. You must know that. That first night at the Pouso da Rainha I insulted you because I was enraged to find myself on fire for a woman I believed to be worthy only of contempt. I saw your damp hair and great frightened eyes, the dressing-gown which clung to your breasts and, *Deus me ajuda*, I could have stepped across my brother's bleeding body and kissed you until you cried for mercy.'

Kate's breathing quickened as she listened, and his eyes dropped involuntarily to the hurried movement of her breasts before he turned away sharply, his jaw clenched. 'I want you now, also,' he said harshly. 'After last night I know I shall never stop wanting you. But, to answer your question, I believe that what happened then has changed both our lives, whether we wish it to or not. After Pascoa I had vowed never to think of marriage again. Now, all is different. Now, Kate, I most earnestly believe you and I should marry.'

There was silence as Kate waited for him to say something more. When he didn't a little flicker of hope inside her guttered and went out.

'Since we seem to be holding a discussion more relevant to the last century than the modern present,' she said bleakly, 'please let me say that I'm sensible of the honour you do me, Senhor Vasconcelos, but I must refuse your proposal. In this day and age men don't marry women because—because they've made love together once. Not where I come from, anyway.'

'You refuse?' he said, his eyes lit with sudden heat. 'Do you know what you are saying?'

'Yes. I'm saying no.'

Luis stood with both fists clenched, then with a muttered curse he reached for her, pulling her into his arms. He thrust one hand into her hair and slid the other low down her spine to bring her hard against him. Kate tried to pull away, but he uttered a triumphant little laugh and crushed his mouth against hers. She fought to remain passive, but it was useless. At the first contact with his aroused body her lips parted in gasping response to the tongue which importuned so sweetly that she shivered in his arms and he picked her up and laid her on the sofa, then dropped on his knees beside her to bury his face against her breasts.

'Tell me again you do not want me,' he demanded thickly.

'I can't, I can't! But wanting isn't anything to do with marrying.'

He raised his head to stare incredulously into her tear-wet eyes. 'What *loucura* is this, *querida*? If people did not desire each other the human race would die out.'

'Marriage is more than just bed,' said Kate, and with every last ounce of will-power she possessed she pushed him away and sat upright, sniffing as she smoothed her hair with a shaking hand. She forced herself to meet the angry gleam in his eyes. 'You and I, Luis, are quite literally worlds apart in birth, nationality, upbringing, our outlook on life. We speak a different language. What chance of success could we possibly expect from marriage with all that between us?'

Luis stared at her in angry disbelief, hauteur in every line of him as he listened to her refusal. 'You are saying you do not want to marry me?' he demanded.

Kate turned away, her shoulders drooping. That, she thought despairingly, was not at all what she was saying. She would have said yes without a moment's hesitation if his proposal had been for different reasons. But Luis Vasconcelos had once told her very plainly that marriage was no part of the future he envisaged for himself. To have him change his mind with some antiquated idea of making an honest woman of her was totally unacceptable—even amusing in a tragic sort of way.

'You smile.' Luis eyed her malevolently. 'You find me laughable in the role of suitor, perhaps?'

'No.' Kate shrugged. 'We Brits have a peculiar sense of humour, that's all.'

He waited expectantly, but as Kate showed no signs of explaining he shrugged. 'It is time for me to leave, I think.' He stared down at her sombrely. 'I have no luck with those ladies I wish to marry, *não é*? Pascoa preferred César—wisely so, *sem duvida*. While you, Catherine Ashley, fear to link yourself with a foreigner. For is not that how you think of anyone born beyond the shores of your tiny little island?'

Kate got up slowly, wincing as various parts of her anatomy throbbed with the bruises of the night before.

'You are hurt?' he asked quickly.

'No. Just bruised and battered—you must be, too.'

'*É verdade*. But it is my self-esteem which suffers most.' He gave her a twisted smile. 'It is bad for a man's machismo to know he falls short of a lady's requirements as a lover.'

Kate frowned. 'That's not true, Luis. What happened between us was truly miraculous——'

'Not so!' he said swiftly. 'If it was the miracle you say why will you not marry me?'

Kate sighed despondently. 'Perhaps I want a miracle of a different kind, Luis.'

He frowned blackly. 'I do not understand.'

'I know. That's part of the problem.' Kate shrugged. 'Never mind. I'll be gone soon. In a little while you won't remember my face, let alone the fact that I refused your proposal.'

'This last, if nothing else,' he said cuttingly, 'will keep your memory fresh for me, Kate. Solely because it is only the second time in my life that I have been denied something I desire.'

His words stung like salt on an open wound, but Kate concealed her pain proudly as she held out her hand. 'I don't suppose we'll meet again for the remaining time I'm here, so I'll say goodbye now.'

Luis raised her hand to within an inch of his lips, in the formal, meaningless salute he'd never offered her before. '*Adeus*, Kate. May good fortune be yours, always.'

'*Igualmente*, Senhor Vasconcelos.' Kate pinned a smile to her stiff lips. 'Is that right? Claudio's been teaching me a few words of Portuguese.'

Any hope that they might have parted in amity vanished with the mention of Claudio. Luis took his leave with a formality which chilled Kate to the bone, keeping her rooted to the spot in the *sala* as he left instead of seeing him to the car. Enough, she thought numbly, was enough.

CHAPTER ELEVEN

FORTY-TWO days, seven hours and twenty-five minutes after shaking the red dust of Vila Nova from her shoes forever, Kate let herself into the small basement flat in Bayswater, poured herself a glass of ice-cold mineral water and threw herself on the plastic-covered sofa with a sigh of relief. So ended another, frenetic day of selling end-of-season bargains to women with wardrobes depleted by the long hot summer.

It was high time, Kate reflected, depressed, that she stopped mourning for Luis, and did something constructive about her future. Since leaving Brazil she'd been merely treading water in a sea of depression, but now something had to be done. Her tenancy of one of the bedrooms in the flat would expire in three weeks when its owner returned from teaching abroad. Kate viewed the prospect gloomily, then brightened at the thought of two whole weeks of peace to think. Annabel, the other occupant of the flat, had this very day taken off on her annual holiday.

Kate finished her drink, then switched on the answering machine while she inspected the fridge to see what delights were in store in the way of supper. The first message was from Annabel, telling Kate that the electricity bill had been paid, and to be a good girl all on her own.

Good! thought Kate wryly. Fat chance she had to be anything else.

The second message was from her mother, asking Kate to ring. Their conversation later was the usual exchange of mild banter which Mrs Ashley employed to hide her anxiety over Kate's lack of interest in life since her return from Brazil. It ended, as always, with admonitions about eating properly, a discreet enquiry about finances, and a request to come home for the weekend as soon as Kate could manage it.

She could manage it perfectly well this very weekend, thought Kate guiltily. But she wasn't going to because as yet she had no answers to the questions her parents were entitled to ask about their daughter's intentions regarding the future.

Tony rang while Kate was eating her supper, to inform her he was off to Greece on another teaching stint a few days later.

'Come out for a farewell drink,' he suggested.

'If I do will you promise not to lecture me about giving up my job with the language school?'

'Now, would I do that?'

'Only every time I see you.'

'OK, I promise. Tell you what, I'll round up some of the crowd and we'll have a jolly evening.'

As promised, the get-together was lively, but Kate, to her dismay, found herself wondering halfway through the evening why she'd agreed to be part of it. Tony was the only one to notice how quiet she was, and took her aside at one stage for a private little chat.

'You look a bit peaky, love,' he told her.

'I'm fine. More's to the point, how are you?' asked Kate, changing the subject. 'Throat all right?'

Tony followed her lead tactfully, assured her he was in the pink, then insisted she went back with some of the others to his place for coffee.

'I don't know,' hedged Kate. 'I've got to be up early tomorrow——'

'Oh, come on, Kate—I won't see you for ages after tonight.'

As the group strolled from the Underground to Tony's place later a man materialised in front of them in the twilight. For a split second Kate's heart turned over in her breast. Then Tony shouted 'Claudio!'in glad surprise, and turned to grab her by the arm to greet the grinning young man, who for a moment in the deceiving dusk had looked enough like his brother to give Kate the shock of her life.

'Miss Kate,' said Claudio joyously, and wrung her hand with painful enthusiasm while Tony clapped him on the back, made a round of introductions, then invited him in to cram into the sitting-room with the rest in the terraced house Tony shared with two other men. It took Kate a very long time to recover from the shock of believing Luis had come to seek her out. Not that it was new. Several times lately she'd imagined she'd seen him in the street. The hallucinations were painful, and no help at all with her struggle to get over him.

What a dope, she thought bitterly, as she answered Claudio's eager questions as honestly as she could. The other girls in the group listened in shamelessly as they eyed Claudio's handsome young face with open admiration.

'Glory be, Kate,' said Sally Keyes, who'd read English with Kate at university. 'What a hunk!'

'He's a very nice boy,' said Kate, and gave her friend a reproving look. 'And very young, Sal. So go easy on him.'

Kate felt amused by the naked envy in her friends' eyes as Claudio finally managed to isolate her in a corner to talk to her alone.

'I have something for you,' he announced, and handed her the parcel he'd been guarding.

Kate looked at it, her heart thumping madly.

'Open it!' he urged, smiling his devastasting smile. 'It does not contain a bomb, Miss Kate.'

'Just Kate will do now, Claudio,' she said. 'I'm not your teacher any more.' She untied the string on the parcel gingerly, managing to summon up a bright smile as she found that it contained a beautifully knitted sweater from Connie, with an accompanying note.

> Thought you might need this for the long winter nights. Hope the messenger delivers it safely. Much love, Connie.

'How—how lovely,' said Kate, almost choking on the knot of disappointment in her throat. 'Thank you for bringing it, Claudio. How did you know where I'd be tonight?'

'Tony told me,' said Claudio, looking surprised. 'He said you would be returning with him at this hour.'

Kate looked up with raised eyebrows at Tony, who grinned unrepentantly across the crowded room.

Claudio, it seemed, had been working in the London office of Minvasco for almost a week. 'I have worked like a *burro*, Miss—Kate,' he said, looking injured. 'Luis works me like the mule.'

Kate stared at him. 'Is—is your brother in London too, then?'

'*Pois é.* He came before I. He has been in London for two weeks now, and stays to make sure I work hard!'

Two weeks, thought Kate sickly, as she did her best to laugh and joke and behave as though nothing in the world was wrong. After half an hour she gave up and asked Tony to ring for a taxi.

'Are you all right, Kate?' he asked in an undertone.

'I'm fine!' she said in a fierce whisper. 'Why shouldn't I be?'

'No reason, no reason,' he said, backing off. 'Connie sent me a sweater too, by the way.'

'She's a sweetie, isn't she?' Kate sighed. 'I miss her a lot.'

Tony regarded his shoes with intense interest. 'She seems a bit, well, anxious about you, Kate.'

'Anxious?'

'Mmm. Asked me to keep an eye on you. But I can't now I'm going to Greece.'

Kate regarded him with resignation. 'I'm perfectly all right, Tony. *You* got sick, not me.'

He looked up at her with troubled blue eyes. 'It was worse for you, with the kidnapping—and so on. You've never been quite the same since.'

It took several minutes of wearying reassurance, followed by pleas from Claudio for a dinner date one evening, before a taxi arrived to let Kate escape. It seemed forever before she was alone in bed, giving way at long last to the tears she'd never allowed herself to shed since her return from Brazil.

After meeting Claudio Kate lived in a state of tension which took away her appetite and gave her narrow face a large-eyed look which caused comment from the girls who worked alongside her in the Oxford Street store. Each evening she burst into the flat in a frenzy of anticipation, then needed a good hour to recuperate from the fact that no deep, ravishingly foreign voice had left a message for her on the answering machine.

You, Kate Ashley, are a fool, she told herself on the third evening. Luis Vasconcelos has no intention of contacting you, and the sooner you get used to the idea the better. Nevertheless the fact that he was in the same city, even the same country, was tearing her nerves to pieces.

Kate was in her dressing-gown, drying her hair after a shower, when the buzzer on the door intercom rang.

'Yes?' she said curtly into the receiver.

'Kate?' said the longed-for voice. 'It is Luis Vasconcelos. May I see you for a moment?'

Kate stood, receiver in hand, feeling as though every last drop of blood she possessed were draining from her veins.

'Kate?' said the voice in her ear. 'Is that you? Are you there?'

'Yes,' she said slowly. 'I'm here.'

'Then will you let me in, *por favor*?' I will not keep you long.'

She hesitated. 'Very well. But only for a moment.' She pressed the release button for the front door, cursing because there was no time to dress properly. At the sound of the bell she gave a despairing look in the mirror, tied the girdle of her dressing-gown tightly round her waist, then went to let her visitor in.

When Kate opened the door Luis stayed outside in the dimly lit basement hall, just looking at her in a silence which went on for several unbearable moments. He looked haggard but elegant as always in a dark blue suit and striped shirt, but with a shadow of stubble along his jaw. There were matching shadows beneath his tawny eyes, and he looked older and thinner and a great deal more remote than the Luis she remembered.

'*Como vai*, Kate?' he said at last.

She gave him a little nod of greeting, afraid to trust her voice as she opened the door wider and motioned him inside.

Luis looked around him, his eyes taking in every detail of the low-ceilinged room, the cheap, functional furniture, the plants in pots in the large bay window looking out on a railed area with stone steps leading up to pavement level.

'So. Here is where you live,' he said quietly.

She shook her head. 'No. This is where two friends of mine live. I'm just sub-letting a room for a while until one of them gets back from abroad.'

'And the other? Where is she—or he?'

'*She* is away on holiday at present.' Kate bit her lip, wondering if she ought to have let that particular cat out of the bag. 'Can I give you a drink? There's some wine in the fridge.'

Luis shook his head, putting the overhead light in some peril. 'You are kind, but no. I have not come here for a drink.'

What had he come for? thought Kate as she waved him to a chair. 'Do sit down, at least.'

Luis obeyed, sitting in one of the upright chairs ranged round the glass-topped table in the bay window. 'It is strange,' he remarked. 'You are thin and look tired, yet you are very brown.'

'There's a little garden outside in the back, between this flat and the one at the rear. It's been a good summer this year. I've spent my spare time sun-bathing.' Kate perched uneasily on the edge of the sofa. 'You don't look so wonderful yourself, if it comes to that.'

He shrugged. 'I am working very hard.'

'Claudio said you'd been in London some time.'

'That is true.' He took out his cigar-case. 'You permit?' When she nodded he lit one of the thin, dark cigars Kate remembered so well, and said no more until blue smoke added to the barrier between them. 'I wished to contact you before,' he said, regarding the glowing tip of the cigar.

'Why didn't you, then?' asked Kate quietly.

His eyes met hers. 'You ask me that, who rejected my proposal of marriage?' His mouth twisted in a bitter smile. 'I feared you might close your door in my face.'

Kate's chin lifted. 'So why have you come?'

'Because I return to Vila Nova soon, and Connie requested me to visit you to make sure all was well. I would not dare to go back without carrying out her wishes.'

'Oh! I see. Tell her I'm fine. Just fine.'

He looked at her searchingly. 'She wishes to know if you will teach again.'

'Yes. Yes, I will.' Kate's eyes narrowed. 'But in a different way. I'm—I'm going to put my training to full use and teach children.'

'You have a post?' he asked sharply.

Since Kate had only that moment realised, with blinding certainty, exactly what she intended to do, she shook her head. 'No. But I hope to have one soon.'

'I see.' He looked away. 'Claudio says you were very happy with your friends the night he met you.'

'I was with friends, certainly.'

'Were you *not* happy with them?' he asked carefully.

She thought it over. 'Happiness is a relative kind of thing. I wasn't *unhappy*.'

'Will you be sorry to leave your friends when you go away to teach?'

'A little, naturally. But our paths are bound to lead us all in different directions sooner or later.'

Luis said nothing. He sat regarding the tip of his cigar in silence, while Kate, her mind in a tumult, kept her eyes on the toes of her worn espadrilles in despair. Why had he come? Surely not just because Connie had asked him to? And now he was here, only feet away from her, she couldn't find a thing to say. How could she tell a man how much she loved and missed him when he just sat there, as still and formidable as one of *Aleijadinho's* statues in Congonhos? She glanced surreptitiously at her watch.

'You wish me to leave?' asked Luis, rising.

'No!' Kate sprang to her feet precipitately. 'Don't go—not yet.'

He looked down at her broodingly, then winced as the cigar in his fingers burnt down far enough to sear his skin.

Kate rushed to get a saucer for him to stub out the smouldering cigar butt, then took his hand in hers to inspect the burn.

'Does it hurt?' she said anxiously, then recoiled as Luis snatched his hand away.

'No. It is nothing.' Veins stood out on his forehead as he swallowed convulsively.

'Let me run it under the cold water——'

'No!' he howled. 'Do not touch me.'

Kate straightened her shoulders with immense dignity. 'I'm sorry you find my touch so repellent. I knew you were no longer interested in me, of course——'

'Interested!' He closed his eyes like a man in prayer. 'Santa Maria, you English express yourself in strange ways.' His eyes opened to spear her with a look which sent Kate backing away. 'If this word repellent means I do not like your touch, then you are wrong. Dangerously wrong.'

Kate's mouth dried at the note in his voice. 'Are you sure you won't have a drink?' she said in a strangled voice.

'I do not *want* a drink,' said Luis, through gritted teeth. He scowled at her. 'Ever since Claudio met you the other night all I hear is Miss Kate this, Miss Kate that! How beautiful you looked, how happy you were with your friends. I did not mean to come to London. There was no necessity for this. Julio Alves could have overseen the opening of the new office. But no! I insisted I must do it myself.'

Kate ran the tip of her tongue over her dry lips, hugging her arms across her chest. Did he mean that he'd come because he wanted—even needed—to see her? she wondered hopefully.

'Do not do that!' he ordered.

'Do what?' she asked, mystified.

He made an impatient gesture. 'That with your tongue.'

Kate flushed scarlet. 'I can't do much right, can I?'

Luis eyed her sardonically. 'You could have done much that was right, that night at Casa Londres. But you would not. You refused me as a husband.'

'Who wouldn't refuse an offer made out of some archaic sense of duty?' she snapped.

He gave a short, mirthless laugh. 'Is that what I did? Then why, Senhorita Catherine Ashley, have I travelled six thousand miles from *minha terra*, the place where I was born, just to meet with you again?'

Kate smiled scornfully. 'Good question, since you've been here for weeks without making any effort to contact me! How should I know why?'

He folded his arms across his chest in mocking imitation. 'I, Luis Vasconcelos, *Patrão* of Minvasco and head of my family, am not accustomed to rejection. I did not take your refusal lightly, you understand. So I told myself I would demonstrate how strong I could be, how unconcerned by your response to my proposal. I would come to London, ah, yes, but I would make no attempt to meet you. So. I worked hard here, all through weary hours much hotter than I expected in your country, and told myself I had conquered the desire to see you. I would go back where I belonged and never think of you again.'

'What changed your mind?' asked Kate angrily. '*I* didn't ask you to come here!'

He frowned. 'You did not? But Claudio told me you wished to see me.'

Kate glared at him in outrage. 'I said no such thing. Your darling little brother was playing some kind of joke on you—*and* on me.'

Luis eyed her in very obvious disbelief. 'You did not ask him to give me a message?'

'No, I did not,' said Kate raggedly. Then she let out a long, unsteady sigh and looked at him squarely. 'But I'm very pleased to see you, Luis,' she whispered.

It was possible to hear a pin drop in the room for some time after she'd spoken. Luis stood still, his face utterly blank as he regarded her in silence for so long Kate couldn't stand it.

'So you can tell Connie I'm fine,' she said with a sudden rush. 'Thank you so much for making time to see me.'

Luis uttered an odd, stifled laugh and drew her gently into his arms. 'Enough of this *bobagem*, Kate. You know well that all I want is this.' And his mouth found hers in a way which told her without words exactly why he'd come and exactly why he'd stayed, the reasons blindingly obvious to both of them the moment their lips met.

This, thought Kate, dazed, is why I was born. There was no point in trying to salvage her pride by resistance. At the first touch of his tongue against hers her lips parted eagerly. She stood on tiptoe to lock her arms about his neck, not caring a bit that Luis was holding her tightly enough to endanger her ribs, because when he raised his mouth a fraction it was only to whisper words whose meaning was quite clear, even though he spoke in his own language.

'*Eu te desejo, meu amor,*' he said, in a tone which made her tremble. '*É eu te amo.*' He laid his cheek against her hair. 'And this time, little *estrangeira*, I will translate to prevent any misunderstanding. I said that I desire you, but also that I love you. I love you with all my heart and soul, *querida.*'

'Oh!' said Kate, the blood rushing to her face as he put her away a little so that he could look at her.

'Is that all you can say?' he mocked, smiling triumphantly as he picked her up and sat down with her on his knee on the sofa. 'Surely it is only polite to tell me if my feelings are returned?'

'Oh, yes—in full!' She threw her arms round his neck and kissed him with such fervour that it was a long time before any conversation was possible. It was much later, after a great deal of intimate, feverish endearments had been exchanged, before they could talk with any coherency. Luis shifted Kate so that she lay against him with her head on his shoulder, both his arms locked securely about her as they savoured the joy of being together after the painful weeks of parting.

'It is a great coincidence, *não é,*' murmured Luis against her cheek, 'that tonight you are dressed as you were that first night, except for your feet, which were bare.'

'You remember that?' breathed Kate in astonishment.

He slid a caressing hand down her satin sleeve. 'It is a picture which lives with me constantly. I wanted you from the very first moment, even when I thought you were Sofia. When I learned your true identity I fought to control my feelings for the English *professora*. I knew that with you there could only be marriage. And this I did not want at first, you understand. I did not wish to be hurt again. So I suggested a different kind of relationship, to my shame. But after we spent that terrible, beautiful night together I knew I would never know happiness again if I could not have you for my wife. But you refused me.'

Kate touched a hand to his cheek. 'Not because I wanted to. All you had to say was that you loved me, Luis.'

He sighed, turning his mouth against the palm of her hand. 'I did, many times, that night we were locked up together, *amada*. But in my own language. What a fool I have been.'

'Never mind—you can tell me you love me ten times a day from now on to make up!' Kate grinned suddenly. 'I certainly didn't care much for *you* the first night we met. I thought you were an absolute monster!'

He laughed softly, and began to caress her delicately. 'And now?' he whispered against her mouth.

'I still think you're a monster,' she said, moving restlessly beneath his touch.

'Why, my heart?'

'To stay away from me until now.'

'How can I change your mind?' he asked, a certain note in his voice raising the hairs along her spine as he slid his lips over her cheekbones and along her jaw until she was trembling.

'You could love me,' said Kate simply.

Luis swallowed hard. 'I do love you, *carinha*.

'I mean you could *make* love to me.'

He held her cruelly tight, rubbing his cheek against her hair. 'There is something I must say first, Kate.'

Kate smiled at him with confidence inspired by the powerful feeling she knew was almost vanquishing him.

'Let me say it. Luis—will you marry me? Please?' She dropped her lids modestly. 'I thought I'd save you the trouble a second time.'

He stared at her incredulously, then let out a joyous laugh. 'Oh, *menina*! What a liberated English lady! But thank you, Senhorita Ashley. I am deeply honoured by your proposal and accept with much, much joy.'

'Should I have gone down on one knee?' she asked demurely, batting her eyelashes at him.

Luis caught her against him fiercely. 'No, *querida*. You did not even have to ask, because I was just about to say that this time I would not take no for an answer.'

She leaned back in his arms, frowning. 'Being foreign and chauvinistic and all that, Senhor Vasconcelos, would you have preferred me *not* to ask?'

'No! I am so very touched that you felt able to do so,' he assured her, then sighed.

'What's the matter?'

'Now that you have promised to be my wife it is not easy to—to force myself to go, to leave you here alone.'

'You could stay.'

'I cannot, *linda flor*. Claudio knows that I am here. If I do not return to the hotel he will think I have shared your bed.'

Kate smiled mischievously. 'You could have been sharing my bed any time this evening!'

Luis eyed her with mock severity. 'But I have not. And since you are now my *noiva* I will treat you with the respect such a lady merits.' He raised her hand to his lips. 'The first time we made love together, Kate, was a time born of desperation and need. The next time will be on our wedding night when all will be as perfect as it is possible for me to arrange for you, *querida*.'

Kate thought that over. 'Does that mean we must be married in Brazil?'

Luis looked shocked. '*Pois não!* Your parents will wish you to be married here, naturally.' He smiled triumphantly. 'If you permit there could be a civil ceremony here as soon as possible by special licence, then a church wedding in Vila Nova when we return.'

'Two weddings! We'll be well and truly married, that's for sure,' said Kate with a chuckle, but there was no answering smile on the haggard, handsome face of her lover.

'It will be for life, Kate,' he said softly. 'Once I have you I will never let you go.'

'A very satisfactory arrangement,' she said unsteadily, her eyes falling before the look in his. She moved closer, aiming a kiss at his roughened jaw. 'Luis, what do you expect me to do after we're married?'

He looked blank. 'Do? I do not understand.'

'Well, there's no getting away from the fact that you and I come from very different backgrounds with different ideas on a lot of things. We're bound to have to make compromises, allowances, for each other.'

Luis eyed her suspiciously. 'So. What are you trying to say?'

Kate smiled cajolingly. 'I just wondered if you'd let me teach in the new school in Vila Nova, Luis.'

He looked startled. 'Teach? English?'

'No. I thought I could take a crash course in Portuguese and do general teaching with the little ones in kindergarten.' Kate smiled cajolingly. 'Until we have some of our own. Little ones, I mean.'

Colour flared along his cheekbones. 'You know I can refuse you nothing—particularly when you say such things to me. You may do as you wish, Kate. You may teach or redecorate my house——'

'Can I?' said Kate, her face lighting up. 'Won't your mother object?'

Dona Francisca, it appeared, had always intended to make her home in Parana once Luis and Claudio were settled.

'When I marry I think *Mamae* will be happy to leave Claudio in my care and retire to the house my father built for her near Santa Caterina. She has family and friends there,' said Luis. He eyed her ruefully. 'Will you object if Claudio lives with us?'

'Not in the least, if you'll let me do something with that gloomy museum of a hall in your house—within reason, I promise.'

'It will be *our* house,' he pointed out. 'And you may do what you wish, *querida*, as long as you live there with me forever.'

Kate bit her lip. 'I'm not always an angel, Luis.'

He laughed and held her close. 'That is good. What man wants an angel in his bed?'

'There's more to marriage than bed,' she said tartly.

'I know.' He gave her a crooked smile. 'But since, for the moment, it is all I can think of with you in my arms, I shall go back to my lonely bed at the hotel, and console myself with the thought that soon we shall be together every night at Casa dos Sonhos.'

'House of Dreams.' Kate sighed blissfully. 'So beautiful, and so apt, too.'

'I can think of an even better name.' He held her close. 'With you to share my life there, Kate, it will be the house of dreams come true.'

Coming Next Month

#3205 FIREWORKS! Ruth Jean Dale
Question: What happens when two blackmailing grandfathers coerce a
dashing rodeo cowboy and his estranged Boston-society wife into spending
time together in Hell's Bells, Texas? Answer: *Fireworks!*

#3206 BREAKING THE ICE Kay Gregory
When hunky Brett Jackson reenters Sarah's life after ten years, he brings a
young son, two dogs and a ferret. His questionable reputation comes, too—
which doesn't make him the kind of guy for whom an ice maiden should melt....

#3207 MAN OF TRUTH Jessica Marchant
Sent to Switzerland to promote a new vacation package, Sally has no idea
she'll have to confront Kemp Whittaker. Film producer, TV presenter, nature
lover and every woman's fantasy, he opposes Sally and everything she stands
for. Can she withstand his assault?

#3208 A KIND OF MAGIC Betty Neels
Fergus Cameron's arrogance makes him the kind of man most women find
annoying, and Rosie is no exception. Admittedly, he can be charming when it
suits him—not that it matters to her. Fergus has already told her he's found
the girl he's going to marry.

#3209 FAR FROM OVER Valerie Parv
Jessie knows that no matter how hard she tries, there's no way to stop
Adrian Cole from coming back into her life. She knows she wants a second
chance with him—but she's afraid of her reaction to her son, Sam.

#3210 BOTH OF THEM Rebecca Winters
Bringing home the wrong baby—it's got to be a one-in-a-billion chance. Yet
Cassie Arnold's sister, Susan, believed it had happened to her. With Susan's
tragic death, Cassie's obliged to continue her sister's investigation. And she
discovers, to her shock, that Susan was right: her real nephew is living with
divorced Phoenix banker Trace Ramsey, as his son. When Trace becomes
aware of the truth, he insists on having *both* children. There's only one
solution, he says—Cassie will have to marry him....
Both of Them is the third title in The Bridal Collection.

Summer Reading
At Its Best

In July, Harlequin and Silhouette bring readers the Big Summer Read Program. Heat up your summer with these four exciting new novels by top Harlequin and Silhouette authors.

SOMEWHERE IN TIME by Barbara Bretton
YESTERDAY COMES TOMORROW by Rebecca Flanders
A DAY IN APRIL by Mary Lynn Baxter
LOVE CHILD by Patricia Coughlin

From time travel to fame and fortune, this program offers something for everyone.

Available at your favorite retail outlet.

BSR